THROW DOWN—OR DIE . . .

A silence had fallen over the street. All eyes were on the two combatants. Gabe settled his body. He had seen Bates shoot. He knew he was both fast and accurate. A very dangerous opponent. Gabe would have to use his head if he wanted to walk away alive.

Gabe noticed that Bates was still watching his left hand. He let his left hand drift away from the shoulder holster. Some of the tension left Bates's body, the gunslick not realizing that by now Gabe's right hand was practically on the butt of the pistol at his hip. Bates started to smile.

By then Gabe was drawing with his right. Too late, Bates clawed for his gun with incredible speed, but his action was too rushed, his timing off. Gabe didn't try to aim. There was no time for that. Holding the trigger back, he slammed the heel of his left hand against the hammer spur, fanning the hammer not once but three times. . . .

LONG RIDER

★ DEVIL'S GUNS ★

CLAY DAWSON

DIAMOND BOOKS, NEW YORK

This book is a Diamond original edition,
and has never been previously published.

DEVIL'S GUNS

A Diamond Book / published by arrangement with
the author

PRINTING HISTORY
Diamond edition/October 1993

ISBN: 1-55773-954-4

Diamond Books are published by The Berkley Publishing Group,
200 Madison Avenue, New York, NY 10016.
DIAMOND and the "D" design
are trademarks belonging to Charter Communications, Inc.

PRINTED IN THE UNITED STATES OF AMERICA

10   9   8   7   6   5   4   3   2   1

CHAPTER ONE

The buck stepped out of a small stand of cedar, moving with a curious mixture of confidence and caution. It was a big animal, a ten-pointer, deep-chested, regal.

Hidden two hundred yards away, Gabe Conrad settled the buck's flank into the sights of his Sharps carbine. He'd already flipped up the rear sight, setting the crossbar at two hundred yards. There was almost no wind. The rifle's massive seven-hundred-grain bullet would fly straight; the shock of its impact should knock the buck right off its feet. Gabe doubted a second shot would be necessary.

He pulled the set trigger, cocking the main trigger. Now just a touch would send the bullet on its way. But he did not fire, and as the moments passed by, Gabe knew that he would not be able to pull the trigger. What he had seen earlier today still bothered him.

Using his left hand, Gabe lowered the rifle's hammer. He stood up, in plain view. The buck saw him immediately, remained standing for perhaps three seconds. Even from two hundred yards away, the tension in its body was obvious to Gabe. Then, with a huge bound, the buck disappeared into the cover of the trees.

Gabe remained in place for a moment, looking at the spot

where the buck had disappeared. Too bad. He was very hungry, and deer meat would have tasted good. But he would not have been able to eat very much of the buck, nor did he intend to stay in the area long enough to dry and jerk the meat.

His mind went back to what he had seen several hours ago. The deserted camp of the white hunters. The stacks of bones, of antlers, thrown carelessly aside. Piles of rotting hides, those not considered good enough for sale. Mounds of stinking offal, left for scavengers.

Meat hunters. That was what men like that were called among the whites. Men who slaughtered every edible animal they came across to provide meat for the white towns and settlements that were cropping up all over the territory. To provide food for fancy restaurants. Hunters who killed for profit, for money, rather than to feed themselves and their families. Avaricious men who would soon exterminate game from these mountains, who would, with their greed, make certain that in the future few would be able to feed themselves from this natural abundance, an abundance that had been providing life for the *oyate nikse*, the native people, forever. As Gabe's people put it, since time began, since the rivers began to flow, the rain to fall, and the wind to blow. Gabe grimaced. If the white men could find a way to capture the wind, they'd sell that, too.

Gabe hiked back over a crest to where he'd left his horse, a big, black stallion. The horse raised its head when Gabe came into view. The stallion was not a pleasant animal; it tended to bite when it thought it could get away with it, but by now Gabe had convinced the animal who was boss. He valued the horse. The black's strength, endurance, and lack of fear, even when gunfire was going off all around it, more than made up for its foul temper.

Gabe shoved the Sharps into a saddle scabbard on the horse's right side. On the left, where he could reach it easily, the butt of a Winchester .44-40 jutted from another scabbard. A Colt revolver of the same caliber as the Winchester rested in a hoister on his right hip, worn butt forward, cavalry style.

An identical pistol was tucked into a shoulder holster beneath his right armpit, suspended butt downward by a spring clip. The bone handle of a long-bladed knife jutted from a sheath sewn to the side of the shoulder holster. The shoulder rig was in plain view; it was a warm day, and Gabe was not wearing a coat. Besides, during the week he'd spent riding through these mountains, he had yet to meet another human being.

Gabe mounted the stallion, then pointed him northeast, the direction in which he'd been heading for several days. Beautiful, wild land lay all around him, with jagged mountain peaks in the distance and rich meadows close up. Nowhere did he see any great expanse of level land. A distinct change from the Dakota prairies where he'd grown up, the endless plains where his people had constantly been on the move . . . a few weeks here, a few there, then down with the lodge poles, everything stacked onto the travois, the whole village mounted on their ponies, ready to move on, to follow the buffalo. Always pushing on. Only during the coldest part of the winter did the People stay for long in one place, living precariously on what they had stored up during the warm days of summer and fall, snug inside their tipis, lazily making love, the men singing songs, telling stories of the hunt and of war, while the women, in the midst of their endless chores, listened contentedly.

Gabe soothed the ache in his empty belly by letting his mind dwell on memories of the old days, on scenes of the hunt, of the endless fight against the tribe's old enemies, the Crow and the Pawnee. Most of all, remembering the closeness among the People, of the way they lived together as a big family. Remembering the warmth of belonging. But the more he remembered, the more the memories hurt, until his mind began to ache as much as his stomach.

Gone. All gone. Gabe was a wanderer now, cut off from his people. He had found it impossible to stay among them, impossible to watch their suffering, their daily degradation. The greatest pain was the knowledge that he could do nothing about it. Many had tried, better men than himself. And

they had failed. Men like Crazy Horse, his friend. Dead
now, treacherously murdered by the white soldiers. And
Red Cloud. Not dead. Not his body, but in a way his spirit,
locked inside a body that was locked inside a reservation.
Red Cloud, the great Oglala warrior, crammed, like the rest,
onto a tiny portion of the vast spaces over which the Lakota
had once ranged. A land they had dominated for centuries.

Gabe grimaced as he remembered his last meeting with
Red Cloud, only a few months earlier. Remembered also the
days, long ago, when he'd ridden with Red Cloud against
the soldiers. "Red Cloud's War," the white men had called
it. One of the few wars the Lakota had won. The war that
forced the army to close the Bozeman Road, the wagon
road, that obscene track cutting straight through the heart
of Lakota land.

To Gabe, those days had been full of mixed feelings, the
thrill of battle, the exultation of victory, but also a nagging,
growing unease, a realization that none of this was liable to
end well. Not for the Lakota. There was the frustration of
seeing fine warriors fail to push through to a final triumph.
Warriors who were too independent, too proud, too filled
with a sense of their own worth to follow the leadership
of a man like Red Cloud. Warriors who would leave in the
midst of a battle to ride back to their lodges, not because they
were cowards, but simply because they were hungry, or bored
with the fighting, or wanted to make love to their wives. No
victory was ever followed up, no lasting gains made against
the white soldiers, who knew one thing above all else. Disci-
pline. An iron sense of purpose that eventually won out over
the careless, aimless bravery of the Lakota warriors.

The last time Gabe had visited Red Cloud, he'd had to
sneak onto the reservation; his appearance made it illegal
for him to be there. Red Cloud had greeted him warmly
enough, but Gabe was aware of the terrible, broken sadness
inside that once-great old warrior. And Red Cloud definitely
was growing old, as much from his imprisonment as from the
passage of years. The soldiers watched Red Cloud constantly,

always afraid that he might break out of the reservation and start another war.

But Gabe knew he would not. A few years before, after a period of fighting that had left too many of the Lakota dead— women and children and old men as well as warriors—Red Cloud had accepted an invitation from the Great White Father to travel East. So that the two could talk, it was promised, as leaders of two sovereign nations.

Red Cloud never told Gabe what the Great White Father said to him. He had talked only of the vast distances he'd traveled, first on horseback, then on the iron horse. Talked of his shock at seeing the true strength of the white world, the hundreds of miles of settlements, towns, cities. The vast numbers of the white men themselves. "As many as the stars in the night sky," Red Cloud had said.

In those great cities were all the machines necessary to make the endless stream of weapons that ended up in the hands of the white soldiers. Red Cloud had returned from the journey convinced that the only possible ending for a war of Lakota against the White Man would be the total destruction of the People. Men, women, children. So he had, on his return, steadfastly given counsel against further fighting. Many of the young warriors, full of fire and igno-rance, now scorned him. But Red Cloud had told Gabe that the most important thing was to see that at least a remnant of the People survived. Perhaps someday, far in the future, there would be a place in this land for the old ways, for the free ways. . . .

A movement off to his left took Gabe's mind away from the past. It was a rabbit, about forty yards away, hopping toward a clump of brush. Gabe pulled his horse to a stop, slipped the Winchester from its saddle scabbard, cocked the hammer, aimed for a second, and smoothly squeezed the trigger.

The shot was a good one, hitting the rabbit near the head, so that the hindquarters were not damaged. Gabe rode over to where the rabbit lay, then dismounted and picked it up.

The body was warm, but was not even quivering. His horse snorted at the smell of fresh blood when Gabe laid the rabbit across its crupper.

A thick patch of alders a quarter of a mile away indicated water. A few minutes later Gabe rode up to a small stream running down from a spring that bubbled clear water out of a cleft in the rocks several feet higher up. Gabe dismounted, tossing the rabbit onto a patch of coarse grass. He spent the next few minutes tending to his horse, unsaddling the animal, rubbing him down with a piece of gunnysack that he carried tucked beneath his bedroll. Since he would be riding on later, he did not remove the animal's bridle, but left him staked out in the middle of the grassy patch, contentedly cropping the tough stems.

It only took a few minutes to gather dry wood and start a fire. By the time he had skinned and gutted the rabbit, a bed of coals was already forming. Going over to the alders, Gabe cut green wood, fashioning two forked sticks, which he thrust into the ground at each end of the fire. He spitted the rabbit on another piece of green wood, then laid the carcass across the two forked sticks, to cook over the coals.

While the rabbit was cooking, Gabe knelt by the little stream to wash his face and hands. Here the water had formed into a still, deep pool. Leaning over the pool, he caught sight of his reflection. As usual, he experienced the usual slight shock. Having grown up among a people noted for their dark skin, straight black hair, and obsidian eyes, his own appearance always surprised him . . . the almost blond coloring of his long sandy hair, his eyes, so pale a gray that they were almost colorless. And even though his skin had been bronzed by years of exposure to sun and wind, it was indeed a bronze, not the rich mahogany-brown so common among the People. He'd been wearing a shirt for months, so he caught sight of pale white flesh at the vee where the shirt buttoned.

His skin, his hair, his eyes, all permitted him to escape the confines of the reservation, to ride out into the White Man's world, a world closed to his Lakota brothers. A freedom he craved, but which also laid on him another of the White Man's attributes—guilt, because he alone could escape, simply due to an accident of birth, of coloration.

Gabe thrust his hand into the water, shattering his image. He washed hastily, then went back to the fire. The rabbit was beginning to burn on the side nearest the coals. He rotated the spit half a turn, shutting his mind to the past. He forced himself to concentrate on his surroundings, the mountains, their beauty, their isolation, the great peace that lay all around him.

When the rabbit had cooked through, he ate hurriedly. He wanted to leave this place, where memories had assaulted him so strongly. Still wiping grease from his mouth, he saddled his horse and rode away.

Where? Which way should he go? He'd had his fill of white towns and cities. He thought of the Shoshone. Their land lay not far from here. Perhaps he would ride there, stay awhile. There were many Shoshone who had heard of Long Rider, the Lakota warrior, men and women who would welcome him, who would let him stay among them for a while. Their chief had made peace with the whites long ago; the Shoshone still lived undisturbed in their ancient land. Mostly, Gabe thought bitterly, because no white men as yet coveted that difficult land of steep mountains and cold rivers.

The day was getting older; long dark shadows ran down from the mountaintops, obscuring valleys. At first Gabe thought that the great cloud of airborne debris ahead was merely a trick of the afternoon light. But within a few minutes he saw that it was something else entirely.

A vast pall of dirty smoke rose from the other side of a range of hills. Gabe realized how much smoke there was when fifteen minutes of riding did not bring the smoke that much closer. It was forty-five minutes later, after cresting a hill, that he was able to see the source of the smoke. As he looked at the devastation spread out below him, his mind recoiled.

CHAPTER TWO

A mine. It could only be a mine. About three quarters of a mile away, in a shallow fold in the hills. He could see a tangle of cheaply thrown-together buildings, some quite large, with smokestacks jutting above them, belching thick smoke. The valley floor around the buildings was a sea of dust and mud.

At the end of the little valley, closest to Gabe, was a collection of smaller, even shabbier-looking buildings, indicating a town, the kind of town that grows up near a mine. And all around the valley, for more than a mile in every direction, lay total devastation. Every tree, all the way up the mountain slopes, had been cut down to provide wood, probably for constructing the buildings, and certainly to feed the mine's boilers.

Gabe sat his horse for several minutes, looking somberly at the scene below. His first impulse was to give the valley and its mine a wide berth, to ride way around the area, then back up into the cool, clean mountains.

However, he could see no way around; the trail led right down into the valley. There were a few smaller trails climbing the slopes around the mine, but not far enough away. It was backtrack for many miles or ride on through.

Gabe decided on the latter. For one thing, he needed supplies. He was low on ammunition and wanted to buy some bacon and a few cans of beans and peaches. Trail food. So he rode on down the slope, noticing that the logged-over ground had begun to erode badly. No wonder there was so much mud below. Although the dry mountain slopes indicated that it had not rained for a while, the valley floor had been turned into a thick soup, partly because of natural runoff, partly because of an overflow of the water that the mine itself used. A sluggish stream ran right through the center of the valley.

When he reached the valley floor, Gabe noticed that the stream's water was a strange color, an orange-green, tainted by whatever processes went on inside the larger mine buildings. Or perhaps from filth leaching out of the huge piles of mine tailings that had been dumped onto the slopes.

Before reaching the buildings, Gabe dismounted. A linen duster was strapped behind the saddle. He put it on to cover the pistol and knife in the shoulder hoister beneath his right armpit.

Mounting, he continued on. The smaller buildings that made up the town lay at his end of the valley. In a couple of minutes he was guiding his horse down a muddy, foul street. Many of the buildings seemed to be rooming houses, long, plain, two-story structures, thrown together out of unpainted lumber, with rickety staircases at the back. Probably housing for mine workers. There was considerable foot traffic, perhaps a shift had just ended down inside the mine.

Gabe headed toward one of the larger buildings, a long, low, warehouse-like structure, with a sign hanging over the front door, proclaiming, GENERAL STORE, and under that, SUPPLIES.

Gabe dismounted in front of the store, careful to step directly onto the boardwalk, rather than have his moccasins sucked down into the thick muck of the street itself, a quagmire, a stinking mixture of mud, horse droppings and urine, and the contents of chamber pots. The wood of the boardwalk was almost as bad, splintered and gritty, with muck ground deep in between the cracks.

While Gabe tied his horse's reins to the hitching rack, he casually glanced around him, surprised to see that several of the men on the boardwalk, and indeed on the far boardwalk on the other side of the street, were watching him intently, perhaps even with hostility. Gabe looked away, not wanting to encourage more hostility by openly staring at anyone. Among the Lakota, staring someone straight in the eye was considered an aggressive act. Gabe had always had difficulty with the White Man's habit of the frank, direct look.

He debated taking his rifles into the store with him, but finally decided against it. Moving quickly and quietly, he walked in through the store's big double doors, which were propped wide open. Inside was a single vast room, its openness broken up by rough-cut four-by-four pillars. Goods were stacked everywhere in such abundance that Gabe did not know where to begin looking.

He moved around the room, locating what he wanted. A clerk stood behind a long counter made of rough-cut planking. Gabe walked over to the counter, stacking up half a dozen boxes of .44-40 cartridges, plus powder and lead for the big Sharps. He reloaded his own shells for the Sharps. He wanted complete accuracy.

He saw that the bacon and some of the canned fruit he was after lay stacked behind the counter. He was telling the clerk what he wanted when he became aware again of an air of hostility around him. Even the clerk was eyeing him warily. Gabe paid no outward attention, wondering if it was his long hair and moccasins. Perhaps there had been Indian trouble lately. Perhaps certain aspects of his appearance were making the locals nervous.

Gabe paid for his purchases. But he'd bought so much, there were so many things piled in front of him on the countertop, that he would not be able to carry them all outside in one trip. He doubted the clerk would help him; the man's manner was still hostile. Gabe lugged the heavy canned food, the bacon, and the powder and lead outside first, stuffing everything into his saddlebags. When he went back inside for the .44-40 cartridges, he saw that more men had come into the store. And each one of them seemed to be staring directly at him.

Gabe picked up the cartridge boxes and started stuffing them into the pockets of his duster; he wanted his hands free. By now, several men had crowded in close to the counter. They were spread out in a half circle between Gabe and the door. All of them appeared to be workingmen, probably miners. Gabe was still trying to ignore the men, when one, a burly man with a thick, tangled black beard, stepped out of the pack and stood facing Gabe, no more than a yard away. "Where you from, stranger?" the man asked curtly.

Still looking down with what he considered courtesy, Gabe murmured, "Far away."

"Hey . . . that ain't no answer," the man growled. "An' look me in the face, damn it!"

"Another o' them hired guns," a second man said. Gabe's duster had fallen open while he was filling its pockets with the boxes of shells. The man had seen the butts of both pistols. "Hung with guns," the man added. "His horse, too. I checked."

"That's right, ain't it?" the man with the beard asked Gabe. "You're a hired gun, come here to shoot us up."

Gabe finally looked up, his gaze meeting the other man's. "I don't hire out to anyone," he said quietly, but his voice was not friendly. Gabe was finally becoming annoyed. The man, startled by Gabe's icy stare, took a half step backward.

"You're a liar, mister," the second man said. "Just too many guns."

Now Gabe looked toward him. This man, sheltered behind the first man, met Gabe's eyes more boldly before he turned to address the men around him. "What say we take care of him now, boys?" he called out. "Before he can bushwhack us when we're alone."

"I said that I do not work for any man," Gabe said coldly, although he felt hot with anger. There were eight or ten men pressing in around him. Two or three had pistols stuck into their belts, some danger there, but perhaps the greater danger lay in the stacks of pick handles, axes, and shovels that filled the store's aisles. If the men closed in on him any more tightly, they'd be able to overrun him before he could shoot more than one or two.

Then another voice broke in, a steadier, more reasonable voice. "Easy, Hank. Maybe he isn't what he looks like. Maybe he's telling the truth."

Gabe's eyes flicked to the side. The man who'd just spoken stood a little apart from the others. Indeed, many things set him apart: his cleaner, neater clothing, most of all, the intelligence in his wide-set gray eyes. He was a tall man, with a rangy build. A good-looking man.

The man with the beard, Hank, the one who'd been baiting Gabe, swiveled a thick neck toward the man who'd just spoken. "You stay out of this, Peterson. You don't never back up the rest of us when you should. If we'd o' got that other gun-hung bastard when we had the chance, Jack Henderson would still be alive."

Still speaking in a reasonable voice, the man named Peterson said, "Just take it easy, Hank. Maybe this fella's just passing through."

"And maybe he's the good fairy," Hank snorted, trying to stare Peterson down. "I say we take care of him right now, work him over, bust his hands up good and proper, so's he cain't bother nobody never."

Initially, Gabe had not wanted to hurt anyone, but he was beginning to wonder if he had any choice. It looked more and more as if it would be either him surviving or these workingmen. He was definitely not going to allow them to rough him up. Obviously, something was going on in this town, something he did not understand. And some of these men, maybe all of them, with the exception of this Peterson, felt that Gabe was on a side other than their own.

Still, Gabe did not want to shoot anyone. Not unless they forced him to. But Peterson had given him a way out. He and Hank were still arguing, with Hank turned halfway around, facing Peterson. Most of the other men had their attention focused on the argument. With the shells now in his pocket, Gabe slowly reached across his body with his left hand and slipped his hip pistol from its holster.

It was Peterson who first saw what Gabe was doing. His eyes widened. "Look out!" he shouted.

Hank, who was standing closest to Gabe, started to spin around. Gabe saw the anger on the man's face, the sudden crazy rage in his eyes. In a moment he would shout out some curse and leap at Gabe, hoping, at this close range, to grab the pistol before Gabe could pull back the hammer and fire. If he was successful, the others would close in immediately. So Gabe, still hoping it would not be necessary to kill anyone—unless there was no other choice left—backhanded the barrel of the pistol against the side of Hank's head, just above his left temple.

Hank bellowed with pain, pressing his hand against the sudden rush of blood flowing from where the pistol had struck. He staggered and was just beginning to fall when Gabe thumbed back the hammer and fired the pistol, sending a bullet into the ceiling. Inside the confines of the store the sound of the shot was deafening, reverberating off the walls. Men had already started to move toward Gabe, but now they stopped in their tracks, all eyes on the smoking pistol in Gabe's left hand.

"I'm walking out of here," Gabe said flatly. "I'd like to go peacefully, but if I can't, I'm going to start killing people."

One of the men let his hand move toward the pistol butt jutting from his waistband. Gabe pointed the muzzle of his own pistol directly at the man's stomach. "Starting with you," Gabe snapped.

The man's hand immediately jerked away from the pistol, his eyes full of startled fear. Gabe swept the pistol's muzzle over the others. "I don't know what's bothering you idiots,"

he said, "but I don't want any part of it. Try to stop me, and
I'll blow the guts out of all of you."

The words themselves were threatening enough, but it was
the way Gabe said them that froze the men and kept them
from gathering their courage. There was a coldness in Gabe's
voice, a deadly certainty that he would indeed kill any man
who tried to stop him.

An aisle opened for Gabe. He walked forward, into the
gap, and when he'd passed through the men, he turned around
to face them, walking backward, pistol sweeping the room.

Hank, groaning, was up on his knees now, his hand still
pressed to his bloody head. "Where is he?" Hank muttered
thickly. "Where is the son of a bitch?"

Gabe backed out the door, into the street. Sliding the
pistol back into its hoister, he untied his horse's reins, then
swung up into the saddle. There was now a considerable
uproar coming from inside the store. "Goddamn, boys!" one
man was shouting. "Let's get at them guns and ammunition.
We'll make that bastard wish he'd never taken their filthy
money!"

Gabe turned his horse's head away from the store, toward
the mine buildings ahead. Behind him, he heard a loud
pounding of booted feet. A backward glance showed a mob
pouring out of the store, onto the boardwalk, most of them
now carrying pistols, a couple with shotguns. Some were
still shoving shells into their weapons, which they must
have taken from the storekeeper. Gabe kicked his horse
into a trot, at the same time letting his left hand reach
over to touch the butt of his Winchester. But he did not
yet draw the rifle from its scabbard. In another moment
he'd be around a bend in the street, out of the line of fire.
He had seen few horses tethered near the store, and if his
pursuers did not have mounts, he'd be out of their range in
no time.

Then Gabe saw more armed men directly ahead. Perhaps
a dozen. Hard-looking men, much harder-looking than the
men back at the store. Somehow word had outrun him. He

was cut off, guns behind him, guns to the front.

Bad odds, but no other thought occurred to Gabe, except to fight. Once again his hand reached out for the Winchester.

CHAPTER THREE

Gabe had the Winchester halfway out of its saddle scabbard when he noticed that the men ahead were not paying much attention to him, but were looking further down the street, at the mob. Their guns were coming up into position, but, once again, they seemed directed at the mob behind him.

He guided his horse to the right, out of the way, close up against a building. Turning in the saddle, he looked back. The mob had stopped in the middle of the street. He saw Hank, blood from his head wound running down onto his shirt, standing a little in front of the others, glaring, not at Gabe, but at the men ahead.

Yes, Gabe reflected, he'd definitely stepped into the middle of something he didn't quite understand. The hate between the two groups of armed men was palpable. Yet there was also fear. Gabe could see several members of the mob shrinking back, lowering their weapons. Not hard to tell why. Most of them appeared to be workingmen, miners. The men ahead had the appearance of professional gunfighters, not only because of the number and quality of their weapons, but also because of the easy, natural way they carried them. Their clothing was different, too, not the work-worn clothing of the men in the mob, but made of finer material, clothing that had not seen hard, grinding wear.

Most striking of all was the air of casual violence about the gunmen, their obvious readiness to fight. Some were grinning wolfishly, eyeing the men in the mob the way predators eye their prey.

As hard a group as they were, one man stood out among the gunmen, a tall man, once probably lean, but slightly run to fat now. Gabe could see the hardness in his eyes, the coldness. He had met killers before. This man had the look of a killer. Worse . . . of a man who liked killing. He was standing a little in front of the others, a Winchester held casually in his right hand. A quick glance at Gabe, then his eyes flicked back to the mob. "You boys goin' somewhere?" he called out.

Gabe turned, saw that Hank was still a step or two ahead of the rest of the mob. Hank grimaced, the hate plain on his face. He gestured toward Gabe, although he never took his eyes off the tall gunman. "We want that stranger, Jennings," Hank replied.

The man Hank had called Jennings smiled coldly. "You want to try and come for him?" he asked, his voice taunting.

Hank scowled, then turned to face the men around him. "Goddamn, boys," he growled. "We was right. That bastard's one of 'em."

"What say we take him anyhow?" a man called out from near the back of the mob. "Take 'em all!"

A growl of assent rose from the mob. Then Jennings stepped forward, two paces closer to the mob. The rifle he was holding was now pointed straight at the men. "Who said that?" he snapped. "Who thinks he can take us?"

The gunmen were fanning out, half-surrounding the men in the mob. The gunmen were outnumbered, but once again the mob shrank back. "Go ahead," Jennings called out. "Try it. We're waiting."

For just a moment the miners swayed forward, their faces full of rage and loathing. Then Jennings fired his rifle, fast, three times, the bullets whistling just over the heads of the miners. The other gunmen raised their rifles; two had shotguns. In the sudden silence, the sound of hammers being cocked sounded unnaturally loud. "Go ahead," Jennings said again, his voice low and soft, full of the anticipation of pleasure.

Some of the miners immediately turned away and began walking hurriedly back down the street, their weapons carefully pointed away from the gunmen. Several stood fast for a moment, then they too turned away, eyes aimed down at the ground. In a few seconds the mob had totally broken up, with men hurrying away as fast as they could move without actually running. Even Hank had retreated.

Gabe turned back toward the gunmen. Some of them seemed disappointed. Jennings had a sneering smile on his face. He was staring fixedly after the retreating miners, the way a mountain lion might stare at escaping prey. "That bastard Peterson," Gabe heard him murmur. "I didn't see him this time. Just that loudmouthed Hank."

He suddenly turned toward Gabe, who was still sitting his horse a dozen yards off to the side. "You," he said. "Follow me."

Jennings turned abruptly and walked away. Gabe considered simply riding off on his own, but the other gunmen were all facing him now. Riding away might not be so easy. Besides, he was curious. What the hell was going on here?

The men more or less closed in around Gabe as he rode after Jennings, who was heading for a looming structure, shaped like a small fort. It was made of heavy logs, with the second story overhanging the ground floor. Loopholes had been cut into the upper story. Yes, a miniature fort.

Jennings was walking straight toward a massive wooden gate. It swung open in front of him; he never slowed, just walked straight at it as if he dared the gate not to open.

Gabe rode in after Jennings. There was a small courtyard inside, with doorways leading off the courtyard. Jennings

walked up to a door. This one he actually had to open all
by himself. He paused in the doorway and turned to face
Gabe. "Come on in," he said.

Gabe shrugged and dismounted. One of the men took the
reins of his horse, a rude thing to do without being asked. He
was immediately called to account when the stallion tried to
bite him. The man danced away, cursing. Gabe took the reins
himself and tied them to a hitching rail. Jennings had already
disappeared through the doorway. The door was still open.
Gabe went inside, his eyes quickly scanning to each side,
looking for hidden assailants, his left hand brushing the butt
of the pistol on his hip.

There was no one inside except Jennings, who was in the
act of seating himself behind a plank desk. Jennings noticed
the closeness of Gabe's hand to his pistol. "A careful man,"
he said. "I like that. You didn't panic, either, when all those
yahoos were after your ass."

Gabe stepped to one side of the doorway, covering his back
with a wall. Jennings smiled, nodded approvingly. Which
irritated Gabe, he had no interest in this man's admiration.
"I'm still wondering," Gabe said, "why those men were
after me."

Jennings face darkened. "Agitators!" he snapped. "Dirty
Reds!"

He reached behind him, pulled a half-empty bottle of
whiskey off a sagging plank shelf, and turned back again to
grab two dirty, smudged glasses. "Drink?" he asked Gabe,
without much enthusiasm.

"No thanks."

Jennings nodded absently, almost with relief, then poured
himself a sizable shot, half of which went down his throat
immediately with a tilting back of his head, an upward jerk
of the glass, and a quick bobbing of his Adam's apple.
"Aaahhh. . . ."

Jennings set the glass on the table, but with his fingers still
wrapped around it. Gabe knew that he would take another
belt very soon; he could read it in the mixture of relief on

the man's face and need. A drinker. That must be what had put the fat on the man's body.

"I think they thought I was one of you," Gabe said.

A moment's surprise showed on Jennings's face. He had been looking down thoughtfully at his whiskey glass. "Huh?" he asked, raising his chin.

"The men in the store. The ones following me. They must have thought I was one of you. One of your gunmen. And that made them mad enough to want to hurt me, maybe even kill me. Now," he asked, looking Jennings straight in the eye, "why would that be?"

Jennings's face darkened. "I already told you. They're Reds. Dirty foreign Communists. They want to take over the mine. And that's why they hate us. We been hired to stop 'em."

With a quick movement, Jennings raised the glass to his lips and drained the rest of the whiskey. Jennings immediately picked up the bottle and began pouring more whiskey into his glass. Gabe had been thinking about what Jennings had just said. Yes, he'd heard a few foreign accents among the men in the mob. English or Scotch accents. "They all looked like ordinary workmen to me," he said.

Jennings snorted. "Most of 'em are. It's the agitators that stir 'em up. Who tell 'em they should get more money, that they have a right to say how the mine's run, down below. As if a mining company can afford to have a bunch of mangy miners telling 'em how to run their operation. Safety, safety. That's all they yap about. Bunch o' cowards. If they want to be miners, they gotta accept the risks. Yappin' about their damned unions. . . . Damned if there'll be any unions around here! Hell, that's a foreign Communist thing. Un-American. If we don't stop it here . . ."

"That's your job, I suppose. The men have a union. You're supposed to break that union."

Jennings smiled wolfishly. "They don't have a union. Not yet. It's just the agitators, whippin' 'em up about a union. Talking strike. Hell, a strike? Here? Not while I'm still breathin', mister! We represent order. That's what we're here for . . . to keep order. Hired by the only people who have any right at all to say what happens to this mine. The owners. The legal owners."

"And where are they?" Gabe asked. "These owners?"

Jennings shrugged. "Back East. Where the hell else would you expect mine owners to be? Out here in this shithole?"

Gabe was quickly losing interest in talking to Jennings. A hired gun. Hired by greedy men. Men who literally squeezed the life out of their workers, drove them until they dropped, paid them like slaves. He'd seen it before, seen it to the point where it made him want to vomit. Sick men, these captains of industry, driven by avarice, the White Man's sickness. Greed. The desire, no, the perverted need, to always have more. No matter at what cost. Cost to the men who performed the actual labor. Cost to the land, the ruin this mine had brought to the land all around it. Ruin to their own spirit.

And if someone got in the way of that greed, if some of the men enslaved by the owners tried to stand up on their own feet and demand better treatment, then the owners were always ready to use their wealth and power to hire men like Jennings, men who would terrorize, who would kill if necessary. An old story. One that sickened Gabe.

He was wondering why he had been brought here. It would have been enough for Jennings and his crew to let him simply ride on. He was considering just turning and walking out the door. Considering, also, that an attempt might be made to stop him. There were a lot of men out there. Armed men. Would Jennings let him go? And if not, would he be able to fight his way out?

The door, already half-open, opened all the way, and a man came inside. With a start, Gabe recognized the man. He'd been inside the store. He'd been one of the men howling for Gabe's blood.

The man seemed surprised to see Gabe here. He glanced at Jennings. "Maybe I better come back later," he muttered.

"Naw, Joe," Jennings said. "Come on in." He smiled. "I see you two recognize each other."

No answer was necessary. Jennings smiled coldly at Gabe. "Joe works for me. On the quiet. That's something you better keep under your hat."

The smile was now very cold. Gabe said nothing as he met Jennings's gaze steadily. He had no interest at all in politely lowering his eyes. No interest at all in pleasing Jennings.

Jennings turned to Joe. "What the hell was all that brouhaha about?" he snapped. "Why were they after this hombre?"

Joe cast a quick, nervous glance toward Gabe. He obviously did not like talking in front of a stranger. "They thought he was one of your boys, Frank. Someone comin' in to work for you. It just kinda boiled up, with Hank doin' most of the boilin'."

Joe glanced toward Gabe, then looked back at Jennings. "I thought they was gonna bust him up bad. But he . . ." Joe looked over at Gabe again. "Well, he . . . just cool as a cucumber, laid a gun barrel up alongside Hank's thick head. Hank went down like a gut-shot wolf, snappin' and snarlin', still out for blood. But he . . ." Once again Joe looked over at Gabe, a look on his face made up partly of admiration, partly of fear. "He let 'em know that any man who made a move for him was dead meat. Froze 'em right in their tracks, then walked on outta there, cool as a cucumber."

"That's it, huh?" Jennings asked. He had by now finished his second glass of whiskey and was pouring a third.

"Well, yeah," Joe replied. Then his face brightened. "Funny thing, though. Peterson, he tried to calm everybody down. Told 'em to leave the stranger alone. Let him ride on his way."

Jennings's face darkened. "Peterson? Yeah. He's the only one of that bunch with any brains. Which makes him ten times as dangerous as all the rest put together. He's gonna have to go soon. Real soon."

He stood up behind the desk. "Okay, Joe, that'll be all for now. Get back out there and see what else you can dig up."

Instead of leaving, Joe scuffed his boots nervously against the gritty floor. "I dunno, Frank," he said, his voice climbing toward a whine. "I think they're gettin' onto me. I probably shouldn't have come here today. I get the feelin' they're watching me. . . ."

"So am I, Joe," Jennings said icily. "I got my eye on you all the time. You know that. And you know you'll damn well get your ass back out there and do what I say."

Joe paled, swallowed. "Sure, Frank," he muttered. "I was just . . ."

"See you later, Joe."

A cold dismissal. Joe nodded jerkily, spun around, and disappeared out the door. Jennings leaned forward, balancing on his knuckles against the top of the desk, looking sourly after Joe. "Some of the assholes you gotta put up with in this business. . . ."

He sat back down again. When he looked up at Gabe, his expression was thoughtful. "Sounds like, from what Joe said, you can really handle yourself. Stay cool in a bad situation."

He suddenly laughed, throwing his head way back, eyes squinted half-shut. "I would have loved to 've seen you layin' out Hank. That loudmouthed . . ."

His head came back down, his face cool again. "I need men who can handle themselves. I'll get right to the point. I'm offering you a job. To help me ride herd on that bunch of rock-grubbin' assholes. I can tell you, the pay'll be good. . . ."

But Gabe was already shaking his head.

"What the hell does that mean?" Jennings snapped.

"Not interested," Gabe replied. "I don't work for anyone. I'm my own man."

Jennings's face had grown very cold now. "Oh, yeah?" he asked quietly. "Well, let me tell you somethin', mister. Shit,

I don't even know your name. Let me tell you something, Mr. No-Name. Around these parts, there ain't no independents. Everybody takes sides, or both sides take off after their hide. I'm givin' you a chance to get on the strongest side. My side. Take it or leave it."

"I already said," Gabe replied, his voice lower now, as cold and icy as Jennings's voice, "that I never work for anyone."

Silence. Gabe and Jennings were eyeing one another intently. A wrong gesture, too quick a move, and the room might have erupted with gunfire. For his part, Gabe knew that he wanted to shoot Jennings. Killing him now would probably save a lot of people a great deal of future trouble. But he knew that if he did, he'd have little chance of getting out of this fort alive. He relaxed. Jennings relaxed with him.

"Well, I'll tell you, Mr. No-Name," Jennings said, almost conversationally, "if you wanna be your own man, I'd suggest you ride right on out of this neck o' the woods."

"My original intention," Gabe replied coolly. "If you and your hired guns hadn't gotten in my way, I'd be long gone."

Jennings waved. "Now's the time to do it."

Gabe moved toward the door. Jennings remained seated. Gabe was trying to keep an eye on Jennings and watch what was going on outside. To his surprise, Jennings smiled. "I like a man with sand," he said, almost jovially. "If you change your mind, come on back. You might like bein' part of a winning team."

"I'll keep it in mind," Gabe murmured, not trying to hide the contempt in his voice. One last glance at Jennings, then he slipped out the door.

All the way to his horse, his eyes roved over the entire fort. No one seemed prepared to bar his way. Indeed, no one was paying much attention to him. He swung up into the saddle, rode toward the main gate. It was closed. Two men were lounging beside the gate, looking up at Gabe curiously. He was about to ask them to open the gate, when a voice came from behind him, "Let him out, boys."

Gabe turned. Jennings had come out of his office, was leaning against the outside wall, thumbs hooked in his gun belt.

The two men jumped up and wrestled with the big wooden bar that held the gates shut. A moment later the gates were creaking open. Gabe nudged his horse on through. Open ground lay ahead. He turned one last time, saw that Jennings was still watching him. "Adios, hombre," Jennings called after him.

Then the gate closed him off from Gabe's view.

CHAPTER FOUR

It was only about five miles away from the mine, but in all the ways that mattered, it might have been a thousand. A meadow, untouched, perfect, tucked within a tiny valley. A clear stream sliding silently past grassy banks. Mountains rising all around, their peaks tinted gold and red by the last light of the setting sun.

When Gabe rode into the meadow, a deer was nibbling bushes about fifty yards away. A rabbit hopped lazily across the grass. Gabe stopped his horse, sat watching the two animals, neither of which had as yet seen him. It was a jay, perched high up in a pine tree, that gave the alarm, a harsh cry that the enemy had been sighted.

The deer looked up. The rabbit stopped its hopping, sat on its haunches, staring straight at Gabe, one ear flopped over. Still, neither animal ran. Perhaps, Gabe thought, they could sense his total lack of interest in harming either of them.

Yes, he was hungry, but he had food. Store-bought food. He nudged his horse forward. As he rode out into the meadow, the deer gracefully bounded away. The rabbit stood watching for another few seconds, then slowly hopped into the cover of dense bushes.

Gabe dismounted. First, he unsaddled his horse, took off all the gear, including the saddlebags, then rubbed the animal down with the gunnysack. Rummaging in the saddlebags, he pulled out a hackamore. He spent a few seconds rubbing the flexible horsehair strands between his fingers. Strong, but soft. He slipped the hackamore over the horse's head. The *bozal*, the lower part, fitted snuggly across the animal's nostrils. If the horse fought the pull of the hackamore, its air would be shut off. But there would be no tearing of its mouth. With the hackamore in place, the horse would be able to eat without having to chew around an iron bit.

Gabe attached a long lead rope to the hackamore, then tied the other end to a tree, leaving his horse plenty of room to roam about the meadow.

It took Gabe only a little while to get a fire going. While it burned down to coals, he walked along the streambed until he'd found a thin, flat rock. He washed it off, then took it back to the fire, where he propped it in place a few inches away from the flames.

He got the bacon from the saddlebags. Taking his knife from its sheath beneath his right arm, he sliced several thick strips from the salty chunk, then laid them out on the rock, which was quickly heating. While the bacon was sizzling, Gabe caught sight of movement, about forty yards away. It was a quail, running its crooked race away from one bush toward another. Gabe walked over to the second bush. Peeling back shrubbery, he looked in at the rather surprised little bird, then it was off again, this time with a whirring rush of stubby wings.

Nothing else in the bush. Gabe walked back to the first bush. A clutch of eggs. He took only two of them, reflecting that the average white man would have taken them all. By leaving some, new quail would hatch, perhaps to feed someone else next year. If some animal didn't find the eggs first.

He tossed the eggs next to the coals, to roast. Only one more item to take out of the saddlebags, a loaf of bread he'd bought at the store. A small loaf, not very fresh, but bread.

He cut a slice of the bread and used it to mop up bacon grease; rivulets of it were dripping from the heated rock. A shame to let it go to waste in the dirt. Although the grass would love it.

The bacon looked done enough. He cut another slice of bread, laid bacon strips on the slice, then scooped the eggs away from the fire. He burned his fingers breaking the shells. The eggs were still a little soft inside. He dumped their contents out over the bacon, then began to eat, from time to time dipping his hand into the stream, for cold, fresh water.

Dessert was a can of peaches. Gabe had already spread out his bedroll. He lay on it now, resting against his saddle, draining the last of the sweet nectar from the can. The White Man had some tasty things to eat. Nothing, of course, like fresh-roasted buffalo hump, but with the buffalo gone, a man had to eat what was available.

The sun had set. The sky was still blue, but a very dark blue. Gabe watched the first stars appear against the velvety sky. He inhaled, smelling the last wisps of his fire, the sweet odor of fresh grass, wetness in the air because of the stream. He heard a light breeze rustling through leaves. A perfect place.

Then he remembered the mine. At one time that valley had probably also been a perfect place. But the hand of the industrialist had fallen upon it. A hand that blighted.

He thought back to what had happened at the mine. Senseless violence. The miners had been eager to hurt or kill him, simply because they were not certain who he was. Then there was Jennings and his men, eager to kill the miners. Kill the men who produced the wealth that enriched the men who hired those same killers. It was a war, not over the possession of land, but the ruination of land. A war over greed. Profits. An unnecessary war. Incredible, that the owners and the miners were not working together, toward the benefit of both. But that was not the White Man's way.

How amazed the People would be when he told them about what he had found here. Then, with a sickening pang he remembered that he would be telling them nothing. All those among the People who most mattered to him, his mother, his wife, his friends, were dead. All dead. Killed by the White Man. Killed by men who looked like him.

He shut off the thought. He had become adept at shutting off thoughts. He pulled off his moccasins, his shirt and trousers, then slid into the bedroll. With the sun down, the night was a little chilly. He was grateful for the warm wool around him. He'd made the bedroll himself, out of some old army blankets, covered over with canvas. Not as comfortable as a buffalo robe, but much lighter and easier to carry.

He had picked, as a place to sleep, a small grassy spot close up against a thick stand of trees and brush. Anyone coming at him through the trees would be hard put to do it silently, and anyone coming over the meadow would be exposed in the open.

He laid both rifles next to the bedroll, along with one of the pistols. The other pistol went into the bedroll with him. There was a patched spot on the bedroll, still with burn marks around it. One night an enemy had snuck up close to Gabe, when, finally alerted, Gabe shot him right through the material of the bedroll. Better to be careful than dead.

He lay on his back, hands behind his head, watching more and more stars appear, until the entire sky glittered with light. The White Man said the stars were distant suns. His own people thought they were souls, spirits, powers, far away. In either case, they were beautiful. So beautiful, that, just before he finally fell asleep, he had forgotten entirely about the mine, the mob, Jennings.

And almost forgotten about those he had lost.

Although Gabe awoke at dawn, he was in no hurry to ride on. He lay on his back, hands behind his head, watching the world brighten from the sun. First the mountain peaks, then the treetops. Before the sunlight touched the floor of the meadow, he was out of the bedroll. He spent a few minutes washing in the stream, gasping at the coldness of the water. He cooked some more bacon, ate the last of the bread. He'd have a can of cold beans later in the day.

His horse, somewhat bloated from grazing, was not eager to be saddled. It puffed out its stomach while Gabe was tightening the cinch. He waited a minute, then kneed the horse in the gut, and while it was catching its breath, Gabe tightened the cinch again. All his gear went into place, the rifles last. Then Gabe swung up into the saddle and rode out of the meadow.

He headed north and east, following the natural lay of the land; the valleys and canyons slanted in that direction. If he kept on, he'd eventually reach Shoshone country, where he intended to try their hospitality.

He'd only been riding for a quarter of an hour when he smelled smoke. Not campfire smoke, but the smoke of something burning that shouldn't be burning. He almost turned his horse around in the opposite direction, but curiosity pulled him along toward the smoke.

He knew that a house was on fire even before he actually reached the site. There it was; he could see it through the trees now, no flames, burned-out already, the smoking remains of what had probably been a small cabin.

Nervous horses milled about inside a pole corral. Gabe halted his mount while he was still back in the trees. He'd seen people. Three men. One man was lying on the ground, with the other two standing over him. The two standing men were laughing.

Then they dragged the other man to his feet. He seemed to be having trouble standing. Gabe watched as one man held him, while the other tied his hands behind his back.

Two saddled horses were cropping grass a few yards away. One of the men walked over to one of the horses, took a lariat from the saddle, then, shaking out a noose, looped it around the bound man's neck. He pointed at a tree about thirty feet away. They began marching the bound man toward the tree.

A hanging. They were going to hang the bound man. Gabe was close enough so that he thought he recognized the man, but not close enough to be certain. So he rode out into the open, heading straight toward the three men.

They did not notice Gabe until he was only about twenty yards away. One of the men either heard him or caught sight of him out of the corner of his eyes. He spun around, settling down into a crouch, his right hand resting on the butt of a pistol that rode low on his hip. "What the hell?"

Gabe had stopped his horse. He was careful to make no moves toward his own weapons. "Just passing by," he said quietly.

The man straightened a little, although his hand was still near his gun. The other man with him had hold of the bound man's shoulder, but was watching Gabe intently. The man with his hand near his gun rasped, "Well, maybe you better just keep on passing by, mister. 'Cause this ain't no—"

The other man suddenly burst out. "Hey, Jake, I know that feller! He's the one Jennings saved from those damn miners!"

Then Gabe knew who they were. He'd seen them among Jennings's men. They were hired killers.

The bound man had been partly facing away from Gabe. Now he turned his head. "Peterson," Gabe said. "That's Peterson, isn't it?"

"Yeah," the one who'd been called Jake replied curtly. "Sure as hell is."

"You're going to hang him?"

Jake looked at him coldly for a moment, then spat in the dust. "Figured it out all by yourself, did ya? Yeah, we're gonna hang the bastard. Got anything to say about it?"

Gabe remained silent. He looked at Peterson. Peterson's face was streaked with blood. For just a moment there was hope in his expression, then he looked away, toward the tree. A thick limb thrust out from the trunk about ten feet up, parallel to the ground.

"Why are you hanging him?" Gabe finally asked.

"None o' your business," Jake snapped. "You said you was ridin' on. Do it, mister. Or maybe you'll be joining ol' Peterson here, for some air dancin'."

The other man, the one holding Peterson, now put in his bit. "Hey, Jake, maybe we oughta . . . you know, Jennings run this clown off for some reason. Maybe we oughta take care of him now. . . ."

Jake started to go down into a crouch again. The other man edged around behind Peterson. Which was unfortunate, as far as Gabe was concerned, because if it came down to shooting, he had as much chance of hitting Peterson as the gunman. At this range it would be all pistols.

"Don't get in an uproar," Gabe said, his voice low and even. "As Jake already said, I'm riding on."

He was already turning his horse. But not taking his eyes off either gunman. Gabe was ready to start shooting if Jake and his friend decided that's how it should happen. But he noticed Jake's crouch relaxing a little, and the other man was coming partly out from behind Peterson. Gabe nudged his horse into a fast walk. "Say hello to Jennings for me," he called out over his shoulder.

Perhaps it was his use of their boss's name that decided the men against opening fire. Or perhaps they didn't relish the risk of getting shot, even at two to one odds. This was supposed to be a nice, safe hanging.

So they let Gabe leave. As he rode, he kept looking back at them, over his shoulder. They were standing in place, watching him go. Only when they were satisfied that he was genuinely leaving did they turn away, back toward Peterson.

Gabe rode another twenty yards, then began turning his horse. The two men had shoved Peterson right under the tree. Jake tossed the free end of the rope over the branch. Gabe started riding back toward them, at a walk at first. When he slid his Winchester from its saddle scabbard, both men had moved away from Peterson. They had hold of the rope end, obviously ready to hoist Peterson into the air.

Gabe cocked the rifle's hammer. He dug his knees harder against his horse's side. The animal began moving faster.

Gabe was still fifty yards away when Jake noticed him. "Jesus!" he shouted, going into his crouch again, clawing for his pistol.

Standing in the stirrups, Gabe shot the hired killer through the chest. Jake cried out and staggered backward, starting to fall. The other man now had his pistol out. Gabe worked the Winchester's loading lever and jacked another round into the chamber. Pressure from his knees caused his horse to veer to the side, so that when the man fired, the bullet burned empty air.

Gabe let out a loud whoop. His horse was running now, zigzagging, as Gabe had taught it. Another shot from the gunman, another miss, then Gabe opened up again, three fast shots, two of them hitting the gunman in the torso, the third in the arm.

Gabe was right among the men now. He saw that Jake was struggling up onto his elbow, trying to raise his pistol. Gabe blew his head off. Then Gabe turned toward the other man. He'd dropped his pistol, but he was still alive, although obviously badly hit. "No . . ." he called out weakly, just before Gabe put a bullet through his heart.

Gabe rode on past, turning his horse in a big circle, looking for any other gunmen who might be hidden nearby. He saw no one. "Were these men alone?" he called out to Peterson.

All this time, Peterson had been standing beneath the limb, the rope draped loosely over his shoulders, now that the free end was no longer in the hands of the gunmen. "Yeah. I'm pretty sure," he replied, his voice shaky. He abruptly sat down, or more correctly, fell down, his legs giving way. Gabe rode over to him and slid down from the saddle. Laying his rifle on the grass, he pulled out his knife and cut Peterson's hands free. Peterson flexed his fingers, flinching as blood began to flow back into them. When Gabe took the rope from around his neck, Peterson said, his voice still weak,

"God . . . I thought I was dead for sure."

"Why did they want to hang you?" Gabe asked.

Peterson shrugged, then winced with pain. "Why?" he asked. "To get rid of me, I guess. Something must have riled up Jennings, made him decide I had to go."

Gabe remembered Jennings mentioning Peterson, back at the fort. He must have sent these two men out this morning to take care of the man he'd called dangerous. Peterson didn't look particularly dangerous, just a large man, whom Gabe had yet to see carrying a weapon.

Peterson slowly stood up. He winced; obviously, his head hurt. Gabe had already taken a quick look at the source of the blood on Peterson's face. A gash in his scalp. The gunmen had probably clouted him over the head.

Peterson stood facing the smoking ruins of the cabin. He shook his head and winced again. "Well, it wasn't exactly a palace," he muttered. "But it was a place to hang my hat. Goddamned Jennings. . . ."

He turned to face Gabe, but when he spoke again, it was as much to himself as to Gabe. "Everybody said I was crazy, living out here by myself . . . because of what's been going on . . . all this trouble. Kinda looks like they were right."

"What'll you do now?" Gabe asked.

Peterson shrugged. "Go stay with friends. Of course, if I had any brains, I'd pull out completely. Get as far away from here as I can."

His face, streaked with his own blood, set stubbornly. "But I'll be damned if I'll let those greedy bastards beat me. Beat *us*."

"Jennings?"

Peterson shook his head. "Jennings is only a symptom. I'm talking about the mine owners. Those greedy bastards back East. They use up the workingman, underpay him, kill him because of their damned greed. Ah, hell . . . I gotta cool off my head."

Peterson walked away toward a small stream that cut by a corner of the ruined cabin. Kneeling down, he stuck his head in the water, scrubbing at his face. Dripping water, he walked over to the cabin. The back wall was still standing. He rummaged around in some debris, came up with some clothing and a towel. "Stink like smoke," he said, grimacing. He dropped the clothing, then took the towel to the stream where he washed it out, then wrapped it, still wet, around his wounded head.

He seemed to be recovering quite well. His movements were more decisive now, surer. When the gunmen had looped the rope around his neck, he must have still been groggy from the head wound. Peterson gestured toward the two corpses. "Gotta do something about them," he said. "Or Jennings and company will try to pin a murder on me. You mind helping me get 'em up on their horses?"

Gabe did not mind at all. Peterson was impressing him more and more. He'd already impressed him back at the store, when he'd spoken up for Gabe in front of the mob. And any man who made Jennings nervous . . .

They laid the two gunmen across the saddles of their horses. The horses were not at all happy with the arrangement— the smell of blood, the deadweight across their backs—but they had little choice in the matter. When the job had been completed, the bodies lashed into place, Peterson went over to the corral, caught a horse, saddled and bridled it, and was ready to ride. "I know a place," he said to Gabe. "About five miles away. You coming?"

Gabe nodded. He mounted his horse and took the lead reins of one of the gunmen's horses, while Peterson took the other. They rode for half an hour, higher up into the mountains. The trail grew more and more narrow, until it was a winding, dangerous track, hanging at the edge of a rocky, brushy gorge. Peterson stopped his horse at a wide spot in the trail, although it was still damned narrow. "This oughta do it," he told Gabe.

They untied the bodies, then tipped them over the edge into the gorge. The corpses fell, bouncing down the shaley slope, disappearing into thick brush hundreds of feet below.

"Hell," Peterson said, "the buzzards won't even be able to find 'em."

The saddles followed, along with all the men's gear. Except for the weapons. Peterson kept two pistols and a rifle. Another rifle he threw after the saddles, because it had initials carved into the stock. "We can use these guns," Peterson muttered. "Gonna be trouble ahead. When they go out to hang people . . ."

Gabe noticed that none of the weapons were offered to him. And he was the one who'd killed the men. Among the Lakota, not only the weapons, but the horses and gear would have been his by right of conquest. But white men figured differently. They called it plundering. Unless it was for a good cause, as Peterson obviously considered his cause to be. Gabe turned away and smiled. How different their ways were, the White Man and the Lakota.

After they'd gotten rid of everything, Peterson led them on in the same direction. They were driving the gunmen's unsaddled horses before them. "We're almost at the top of this divide," Peterson explained. "If we let the horses go on the far side, they'll probably head away downhill. Less chance they'll wander back to Jennings's fort. I figure it's better if those two yahoos just disappear into thin air."

Gabe nodded. "You'd make a good rustler."

Peterson looked at him sharply. Then he laughed. "Yeah. Funny how situations get you doing things you'd have never thought of doing, back in the old, peaceful life."

Gabe shrugged. He'd never lived a peaceful life. Among the Lakota, a man hunted, raided, stole, and made war. That was the warrior's way. The big difference, after the White Man showed up, was that the Lakota spent most of their time losing wars. Except for Red Cloud's War, and the fight at the Little Bighorn. Too few victories to make it any fun. Too many dead warriors. Dead woman and children, too. The White Man made war on entire peoples.

Gabe said nothing of this to Peterson. Instead, it was Peterson who began to talk. Now that he'd survived, he was bubbling with energy. "Came out here a few years back," he said. "Tired of the East. My wife died. . . ."

He grew a little morose. "Didn't have a damned thing left by then. The doctors took it all. So I came out West. Wanted to do something interesting, something different than I'd ever done before. I'd been a lawyer in the old days. Legalized thievery. Thought I'd try making a living working with my hands. Nearly starved for a while. Took a job at the mine. Jesus, that opened my eyes. Got a look straight into the mouth of hell."

Gabe didn't have to do much prompting. Like many survivors, Peterson could hardly stop himself from talking. He told Gabe about conditions at the mine, the low pay, the danger. "They work us twelve, fourteen hours a day. Men get tired, make mistakes, and when you make mistakes in that damned mine, they're usually fatal mistakes. Men fall down the shafts, get buried in tunnel collapses, make miscalculations with powder, then get blown to pieces. All for three dollars a day, even when they work us over the usual ten hours. And now they want to cut the pay down to two-fifty a day. They say times are hard, that we have to economize. We? I bet none of those greedy bastards are selling off their fancy carriages or taking on boarders in their mansions. It all has to come out of our miserable pay."

The more Peterson talked, the more vehement he became. He told Gabe how some of the men wanted to form a union, so they could deal with the owners from a position of strength and unity. He talked of mutterings about a strike, although many of the men were not ready to go that far. They were too well trained in the sanctity of private property, no matter how much it was abused. He told how the owners, frightened, had hired Jennings and his gunmen. "There have been shootings," Peterson said. "There's always a reason given for the shootings . . . sabotage, or catching someone stealing, but what they're doing is getting rid of the leaders among the miners. The ones who are strong for the union."

"Like you," Gabe said. "With the hanging."

Peterson fell silent for a moment. "I guess you're right. Hell, I've been trying to stay out of the way, not get too involved. But from time to time, when something really disgusts me, I shoot off my big mouth. Maybe it's the legal training, but I've been pretty effective, I guess. Which must have put me on Jennings's list. God, now I suppose it's either go whole-hog or get the hell out of the area."

They had by now reached Peterson's ruined cabin. Gabe took his horse to the stream and watered him. Peterson was bustling around, collecting odds and ends of his personal belongings, the few things that hadn't been burned. Then he went over to the pole corral and began tying the two remaining horses on long lead ropes. He was obviously pulling out. A smart move. If Jennings had sent men once, he would be likely to send them again.

"Well, what'll it be?" Gabe asked. "Leave for good?"

Peterson was putting a half-burned packsaddle on one of the horses. "Naw. There's a bunch of fellas who live together, just outside town. Mostly union leaders, the more radical workmen. They've got guns; they're ready to defend themselves. After what happened here today, well . . . I think I should be with them. For lots of reasons."

He turned to face Gabe. "Some of the men I'm talking about were in the mob that went after you yesterday. They'll feel like shit when I tell them how you saved my bacon."

"You musn't do that," Gabe said, shaking his head.

"What?" Peterson seemed genuinely surprised. "But you—"

"Don't tell them about me at all. Just say some men burned you out, maybe that you were in the woods when it happened, that they missed catching you. But don't say anything about me. Nothing that someone might mention to someone else. Nothing that would start making the rounds."

"Well . . ." Peterson murmured, looking at Gabe questioningly, "if that's the way you want it. I can see where you'd be kinda concerned. . . ."

Apparently Peterson believed Gabe was afraid of what would happen if the word got out that he'd shot the gunmen, that killers would be set on his trail. Let him think what he wanted. "It's a promise, then?" Gabe asked. "A promise to say nothing about me at all?"

Peterson nodded. Gabe believed he would keep his word; he seemed to be that kind of man. "I'll thank you now, then," Peterson said, holding out his hand. Gabe took Peterson's hand, shook it. He always felt odd about this white custom, but it seemed to make Peterson feel good. Gabe turned away and mounted his horse. He was pulling the horse's head around when Peterson asked, "Where are you off to, then? Which way you heading?"

Gabe reined his horse in for a moment. "A man offered me a job," he said. "I think I'll take him up on that offer."

CHAPTER FIVE

Gabe rode straight back to the meadow where he had camped
the night before. He had sensed its specialness; now he would
use that specialness. To think. To ask for guidance. Spiritual
guidance.

When he reached the meadow, he staked his horse out, but
did not unsaddle the animal. He took his bedroll from behind
the saddle, lay it on the ground, and unrolled it. Inside, rolled
up, was a heavy buffalo-hide coat, and rolled inside the coat, a
long thin bundle. Putting the coat aside, he lay the bundle on the
grass and unrolled it. Inside was a pipe, the kind the White Man
called a peace pipe, because it was usually smoked at peace
conferences, which were among the few Indian ceremonies
the White Man attended.

Gabe smiled. Spirit pipe would be a more suitable term. To
Gabe, to the People, the pipe was a means of communicating
with the mysterious unseen world beyond the obvious, the
true realities existing behind the apparent realities one saw
each day, with that which one felt, inside.

Gabe smiled again. Only the White Man would bother with
that kind of analysis. A Lakota just knew.

Gabe ran his hands slowly over the pipe. The stem was

quite long, made of a length of hollowed-out willow branch. The pipe's bowl was fashioned of soft red stone. Years of handling had polished the stone to a satiny texture. It felt smooth and warm against Gabe's fingers. It was a special type of stone, a sacred stone, from a quarry in Minnesota, the land where the Lakota had lived long ago, before they got horses, before they moved out onto the Plains.

This particular pipe had great significance for Gabe. It had been given to him by an old Oglala subchief, Two Face. The chief smuggled the pipe to him in an old blanket, just before the army guards took Two Face out to hang him. The pipe had special significance not only because it was a death gift, but because only minutes before Two Face had prophesied that Gabe would soon leave the army guardhouse where he had been a prisoner for so long and once again live with the People.

Yes, they had hung Two Face. A shameful death for a Lakota. The old man had been beaten by an ignorant young soldier before they took him away. All of which Two Face had suffered with quiet dignity. Even though he could not understand why they would want to kill him. Had he not been trying to help the White Man?

A white woman had earlier been kidnapped by another tribe, the Cheyenne. Wanting to make peace with the whites, Two Face had bought the woman, a Mrs. Eubanks, from her captors. On the way back to return her to her own people, Two Face had had the consideration to give Mrs. Eubanks a chance to thank him properly, the way a warrior, a savior, should be thanked. He had laid her on the ground, pulled up her dress, and taken her, as women were meant to be taken. Two Face had been very surprised when, upon reaching the fort, Mrs. Eubanks immediately began screaming accusations at him. Two Face had been hung for rape.

But not before he had given Gabe his spirit pipe. Gabe had kept it near him ever since. He used the pipe often, whenever he felt he needed guidance, although some-times he smoked it simply for the pleasure of smoking.

Laying the pipe aside, on top of its wrapping, Gabe quickly built a small fire. While the fire burned, he picked up a small, soft bag made of doeskin. The bag contained *chanshasha*, his smoking mixture, a combination of tobacco, dried willow bark, and various other plants. A potent mixture, one which tended to move the mind away from the obvious, to that other, mysterious world, toward those forces, those mysteries that lay behind and inside everything one saw or experienced.

The proper ceremonial procedure was as important as the composition of the mixture. Seating himself cross-legged close to the fire, Gabe sat still for a moment, the pipe's bowl cupped in his left hand, his right hand holding the stem. As he sat, he let go of all extraneous thoughts in his mind.

Fire in itself was sacred. Gabe looked into the dying flames, then raised the pipe, presenting it to the spirits of the West, the North, the East, and the South. He then held the bowl close to the earth, and finally, up high, toward the sky.

Scooping a glowing coal out of the fire's embers with his bare fingers, he dropped it quickly into the bowl of the pipe. Wisps of smoke began to rise from the smoking mixture. Gabe raised the pipe to his lips and inhaled. Pungent smoke filled his lungs. He held the smoke inside for a moment, feeling power flooding from the pipe into his body, into his spirit.

Slowly, meditatively, he smoked the entire bowl of *chanshasha*. As the world of time fell away, he let his mind ponder the questions that had been forming since yesterday. This situation with the mine. Jennings said that agitators, foreigners, were causing trouble. That was possible. White men often caused trouble. They seemed to have so many conflicting beliefs, many of which they were willing to die for. Or kill for.

On the other hand, Peterson, a man Gabe found impressive, honest, claimed that the trouble came from the greed of the mine owners. Gabe thought that more likely. Greed appeared to be the White Man's true religion. The gentle man who had been crucified so long ago, the one most white men called their god, the man who had spoken of peace, love, and tolerance, the man who had expressed low expectations for the spiritual chances of rich men, this man was now only an icon, an image, he had been changed into power objects, in whose name the White Man had killed and tortured for centuries. Only greed ran true through white history. Greed and conquest.

But then, perhaps some of these miners—Jennings had referred to them as foreigners, as Reds—perhaps they had their own kind of greed, their own kind of lust for power. Perhaps they hid within their activities another mystery of the White Man's incredibly confusing society.

A man between two cultures, Gabe knew that's what he was. With the smoke still strong in him, he had an image of himself, sitting here on the ground, equidistant between two vast tableaux, one showing the Lakota way, a tradition that ran far back through the centuries, perhaps for thousands of years, basically unchanged, and on the other side, the bizarre, ever changing, dynamic, strange world of the White Man. These two worlds made up the totality of Gabe's experience, his very being.

Gabe shook his head, slowly rose, went over to his saddle-bags, and took out a leather-covered book. The leather had been worn smooth from years of handling. It was a Bible. His mother's Bible. The book she had employed to teach him to read and write English. Her family Bible. All that had remained of her old life, her white life, before the Oglala had taken her.

Gabe opened the Bible. Toward the front was a record of births and deaths. His own birth had been recorded in ink made of berry juice. Gabe Conrad. Son of Adam Conrad and Amelia Reid Conrad of Boston.

Adam Conrad. His father. A man Gabe had never known; he'd died before Gabe was born. Died of that strange White Man's disease—greed for the yellow metal, for gold.

Gabe flipped through the Bible's pages. The margins, the flyleaves, every bit of available space was covered with tiny, delicate writing. His mother's writing. For all those years, this Bible had been the only paper she'd had available. She had used the margins and flyleaves to write her diary, the story of her life after the death of her husband, her capture, the birth of her son.

Gabe had not known the entire story of his birth until later, when he'd read the diary. After he'd pulled it from the smoldering wreckage of his mother's lodge. Just before he'd buried her. He'd read the diary so many times since then that he knew most of it by heart. Yet, he still read it from time to time, went over and over the story of his parents, Adam and Amelia, moving west with a small wagon train back in the forties, heading toward California, the Golden Land. Until a rumor of another kind of gold swept through the wagon train. Gold in the Black Hills, just to the north of where they were.

Fired by ambition, Adam had convinced several others to join him in a dash into the hills to look for gold. The more levelheaded had pointed out that the Black Hills area was sacred ground to the Lakota Sioux. A dangerous place.

But gold fever had driven on Adam and several others. That was why Gabe had hated the memory of his father for so many years. He was a typical white man, who had taken his wife into danger for love of the yellow metal, a man bitten by the White Man's sickness.

The price had been high. His mother had recorded it all in the margins of her Bible. There was a dawn attack by a party of Lakota, the Bad Faces, a subgroup of the Oglala. It was a short, hard fight. Adam leapt from the wagon, from the bed he shared with his wife, into battle. A lance through the chest brought him down. The others were killed just as quickly. Amelia picked up her husband's empty rifle, desperately trying to load it, to fight on alone, until the rifle was taken from her by one of the attackers, a warrior named Little Wound. Instead of killing Amelia, Little Wound, impressed by her courage, had taken her with him, to be his woman, not knowing that Amelia Conrad was already pregnant, had been pregnant for perhaps an hour. She and Adam, waking before dawn, had made love.

And their final act of lovemaking would bring Amelia her only son.

Little Wound would not have minded if he had known; children, from whatever source, were treasured among the Lakota. Their birthrate was low. When the boy was born, there was no doubt whose child he was. Physically, he was all white. But he grew up as a Lakota, in the years before the White Man was a significant presence on the northern Plains. He grew up believing he was one of the People, although as he got older, he was puzzled by the fact that he and his mother looked so different from all the others. His mother was called Yellow Hair, because of her long blond hair. Her son was towheaded during his first few years, with light gray eyes. To a young boy, being different can be crushing. Yellow Hair reassured her son, telling him that their coloring was a sign of divine favor, that the sun had descended and given part of his fire to both of them, to mark them out, to show that they were special to him. Believing, the boy had felt very proud.

By then, Amelia had long since accepted her capture, her life among the Lakota. At first, she had made numerous attempts to escape, but Little Wound had always gone after her and patiently brought her back. As time went on she realized that her son had become an Oglala, that she herself, having lived with what the whites would consider a dirty Indian buck, would never be able to return in honor to the society she had left. She would always be considered, by the ignorant and the bigoted, to be sullied, stained, unacceptable for the company of decent people.

Besides, she had slowly grown, if not exactly to love Little Wound in the same way she had loved Adam, at least to respect him, to be grateful for the way Little Wound had accepted, loved, and treasured her son. Together they had raised him as an Oglala, a child of the Plains.

But as the boy had grown older, Amelia had begun to change her mind about her son. Whites were moving into the area in increasing numbers. The army was becoming a powerful presence. There was scattered fighting. Little Wound and the others were not particularly concerned; the whites were only another tribe to do battle with. A small tribe. Unlike Amelia, they had no conception of the vast numbers of white men further to the east who would flood into the West, driven by their endless hunger for new land. Other people's land. The Lakota, along with other tribes, would definitely fight—they thought they understood fighting—but they would lose. Eventually, the whites would triumph. So many brave Indian warriors would be killed during those hopeless fights. Amelia understood that there could be no other outcome. She was determined that her son would not be among the dead.

So she had begun to teach him from her Bible, not only to read and write, but also something of the white society. So that someday he might be able to fit into that society.

Then she had betrayed him, with the help of an old friend, the mountain man Jim Bridger, also called Old Gabe, after whom young Gabe had been named. Amelia had betrayed Gabe for what she thought was his own good, sent him away to live with the White Man. But the whites threw him in jail at the age of seventeen for defending himself against a cavalry captain, who, drunk, had tried to kill the boy.

Gabe had eventually returned to the People, and then he had witnessed his mother and his new Oglala wife being killed by white soldiers. Afterward, Gabe had spent several years fighting those soldiers. Until the end had come, when there were not enough warriors left alive to carry on the fight. Until, to save the women and children from certain death, even the great chiefs had decided to make peace.

That peace, the locking up of the Indians on reservations, had left Gabe, physically white while inside still a Lakota, lost between two worlds. After the coming of the reservations, the only world left for a man who wished to move as a man, the only world left for a warrior, was the white world. A world, thanks to his mother, of which Gabe had considerable understanding, in which he was able to move relatively well. But still, with imperfect understanding. An understanding he wished to enlarge.

Now he had stumbled across this strange, confusing state of affairs at the mine. A state of affairs that fascinated him, if only as a way to see deeper into the White Man's mind. Something to engage his own mind, and probably his body, because there would likely be fighting.

After all, what else was there to do, for a warrior who had lost his way of life, his people, except to fight for strangers?

CHAPTER SIX

The two gunmen sitting in the squat tower, guarding the fort's gate, saw him coming from a couple of hundred yards away, a tall man riding a black horse. When he got close enough, they noticed the battered slouch hat, the long, sandy-colored hair spilling down over his shoulders, and the fact that he was wearing moccasins, rather than boots. "Hey," one of the men said to his companion. "Looks like that feller who got chased by the mob a day or two back."

"Well, I'll be damned if you ain't right," the other man replied. "Thought at first he was an Injun. Sits his horse like one."

The man leaned forward, straining to see. "Think he's a breed?"

"Naw. Not with eyes that color. Real pale. Never seen a breed with eyes like that."

The other man nodded. "Yeah, you're right. I got a close look at him the other day. Spooky eyes. Don't seem to be nothin' in 'em at all."

"I wonder what the hell he's doin' back here? Jennings didn't seem real happy with him when he left."

By now, Gabe had reached a point a few yards in front of the gate. He stopped his horse, looked directly up at the two guards, but said nothing. It was one of the guards who broke the silence. "State your business, mister."

"Jennings. I want to talk to him."

The two men looked at one another. Finally, one leaned backward, called to some men near the gate. "Open up."

The gate creaked open. Gabe rode into the fort. "He's back in his office," one of the tower guards called down. Then he added under his breath, "It's your funeral, buddy."

Gabe dismounted, then tied his horse to the same hitching rack he'd used the last time he was here. He'd already started toward Jennings's office, when Jennings himself, having heard the noise, stepped out of the doorway. His eyes narrowed when he saw Gabe. But he said nothing.

"About that job . . ." Gabe said, walking toward Jennings. Jennings still said nothing, but Gabe was aware of a subtle change of expression in the man's eyes, a quick gleam of triumph.

"If it's still open . . ."

Obviously, Jennings was going to make Gabe do the asking. Finally, Jennings nodded. "Come on into the office."

He turned and went inside without waiting for Gabe. Gabe followed. Jennings was already seated behind his desk. He did not invite Gabe to sit, but Gabe took a chair anyway. He suspected that showing too much obsequiousness would be a mistake.

"Yeah," Jennings finally said. "A hundred and fifty dollars a month, plus room and board." He smiled. "And all the ammunition you want."

"There's a lot of shooting, then?"

Jennings shook his head. "Just a joke. Most o' these mine muckers are too yella to go for shootin'. We just . . . kinda keep on top of things. Let 'em see we're on the job. That it'd be stupid to cause trouble."

"Sounds kind of tame."

Jennings put his head back and laughed. "Oh," he finally said, "once in a while we have fun and games. Make our own action."

He suddenly grew more serious. "Well? You in or not?"

"I'm in. I could use the money. And the grub."

Jennings got to his feet. "Okay. I'll take you over to meet the boys. Most of 'em are here right now. Not much happening; it's between shifts, most of the miners are below ground. It's when they get time off that there can be trouble, when it can stop being tame."

Jennings was already out the door when he turned back toward Gabe. "Still don't know your handle."

"Conrad. Gabe Conrad."

Jennings nodded, then led the way across the inner courtyard to a half-open door. He pushed it all the way open and stepped inside. Gabe followed. He found himself in a large room with bunks along the walls. Through an inner doorway, he saw more bunks. A dozen men were in the room, some sitting on their bunks, some lying down, others sitting at roughly made tables, cleaning gear or playing cards. They all looked up when Jennings and Gabe came in. All eyes turned to Gabe.

"Boys," Jennings said, "this here is Gabe Conrad. Gonna be workin' with us. Some of you already met him."

That was all. Jennings turned to go, stopped next to Gabe. "Go ahead and move your gear in here. Take one o' the bunks."

Then he was gone. Gabe stood for a moment, surveying the room. So far none of the men had said a thing to him. In fact, there was no conversation at all. Every man there was silently watching him.

He turned and followed Jennings outside. Jennings was already disappearing into his office. Gabe walked to his horse. He could see a stable toward the back of the fort. He led his horse into the stable, stripped the horse of all his gear— saddle, bridle, saddlebags, bedroll—then put the animal into a stall. Using a pitchfork, he pitched hay where the horse would be able to reach it. Then, picking up his bedroll, saddlebags, and his two rifles, he headed back toward his new quarters.

He heard a quiet buzz of conversation as he neared the door, but as soon as he stepped through the doorway, all conversation stopped. Once again, all eyes were on him.

He looked around the room. There were several empty bunks. He picked one near the inside doorway that led into the other room. There was a solid wall behind the bunk, no windows for anyone to shoot through. He walked over to the bunk and dumped his gear onto it.

Chair legs scraped against the wooden floor behind him. Boots thudded his way. Gabe turned to see a man approaching. A big man, with a hard face. "That ain't gonna do, Conners," the big man said. "I use that bunk sometimes."

Gabe looked down at the bunk. From the dust on the top blanket, it had been quite a while since it had been used. He made no move to take his gear from the bunk.

The big man stepped closer to Gabe, until his face was only inches away. Gabe, at six feet two inches, actually had to look up. He had already noticed that the big man was wearing a gun. Most of the men were either wearing guns or had them close at hand. "I said that I use that bunk," the big man repeated, his voice quiet, but not at all friendly.

"That's the way, Ace," Gabe heard one of the other men say. "You tell him."

Gabe looked around the room. Several of the men were grinning now. Others wore completely neutral expressions. Gabe turned back to face Ace. "You want the bunk?" he asked mildly.

Contempt for Gabe's lack of courage flooded Ace's hard features. "Yeah," he breathed out. His breath stank.

Barely shifting his weight, Gabe stepped on Ace's right foot with his left. Ace immediately looked down, and while his attention was engaged, Gabe's left hand slipped inside his duster and came out holding the knife. There was very little movement, but suddenly Ace felt the sharp prick of the knife point under his chin. "Just how badly do you want this bunk?" Gabe asked, his voice still quite mild.

Ace had frozen in place. He tried to look down, to see the knife, but it was so close to his body that all he could see were Gabe's eyes, inches away, looking into his own.

They were the coldest eyes he'd ever seen, eyes that told him this stranger would cut his throat without the slightest hesitation.

Suddenly Ace started laughing. He slowly backed away. "Hey, mister, you're all right," he said, chuckling. "I like the way you move."

There was genuine humor in his expression. Several of the other men were grinning. It had been a test. A test to see what the new man was made of. All of these men practiced a hard profession. None would want a weakling guarding his back.

The mood was much lighter now. A buzz of conversation rose. No one bothered Gabe when he took the bunk's blankets outside to shake the dust from them. He'd sleep in his bedroll, on top of the blankets, but the blankets might protect him from some of the creatures that undoubtedly lived in the mattress.

After he'd stowed his gear and hung his duster on a nail above his bunk, Gabe lay down. He tipped his hat over his eyes, but did not sleep. From under the brim, he surveyed the room, watching the men. A hard group. Fighters. Some had probably taken the job just for the money, others for the chance to fight. Or some because they liked wielding power over the weak. Only a hard man could control a bunch like this. Apparently Jennings controlled them very well.

Gabe had been lying quietly for about an hour when he heard the sound of a bell being rung outside. The men started winding up whatever they were doing. Some were already heading for the door. Ace stopped by Gabe's bunk. "Chow time," he said. "What passes for lunch around here. If you wanna eat, come on along."

Ace's tone was quite friendly. Gabe rolled off his bunk, settled his hat on his head, and followed the big man outside. Most of the others were way ahead. These were bored men, with not much to do except eat, play cards, talk about women, and, if they were lucky, fight.

Ace, walking alongside Gabe, chuckled. "That was a sly move, Conners. Steppin' on my foot before you went for the knife. I gotta remember that one."

"Conrad," Gabe said.

"Huh?"

"Conrad, not Conners. Gabe Conrad."

Ace pursed his lips and nodded. He led the way through another door into a mess hall. There were half a dozen rough plank tables inside. Most of the other men were already seated. A cook's helper was slamming big platters of meat, potatoes, and bread down onto the tables. Men were filling plates. Others were already stuffing their faces.

Ace sat at a table with two other men. Gabe sat to his left. He dragged a plate over in front of him and used a battered fork to extract a huge steak from a metal platter. Then he went after the potatoes.

The steak was greasy, but good. Fresh beef. He'd noticed a number of cattle in a pen near the town. The mining company must have some kind of meat deal going with a ranch. In any case, it was good to eat a big piece of meat again.

Ace's voice cut into his concentration on the meat. "That's some finger you got there."

Gabe turned. Ace was looking at his right index finger. The first knuckle was twisted to one side, so that the tip of his trigger finger pointed over toward his thumb.

"Is that why you wear your gun cavalry style, on the right side?" Ace asked. "So you can draw with your left?"

"Could be," Gabe replied laconically. He'd practiced for years to learn to shoot with his mangled right hand. But no point in giving away trade secrets.

"What happened to the finger?" Ace asked.

"Busted it on a man's jaw."

Among these gunmen, it was exactly the right answer. Ace guffawed loudly. Some of the others grinned. "Woulda hurt less to shoot him," one man chuckled.

Gabe didn't mention that he'd broken the finger knocking out a cavalry captain who was trying to kill him with a pitchfork. Or that he'd been unable to form a tight fist because a moment before, one of the pitchfork's tines had been driven clear through his palm, and that was why the finger had broken. Or that he'd been only a boy when all this had happened. He wasn't here to tell old stories.

Perhaps the men would have liked to ask more questions, but Gabe's laconic answers were warning them off. He knew that each of them wanted to know as much as possible about his capabilities as well as his handicaps, in case they might have to fight him someday. But there was a point at which asking too many questions could actually provoke a fight. So the conversation turned back to cards, women, and booze.

Lunch finished, Gabe returned to the bunk room with the others. Some of the men lay down on their bunks. Snores began to buzz around the room. Gabe decided to sleep while he could, not certain just what his hours might be.

He found out three hours later. A bustle of activity woke him up. He pushed the brim of his hat away from his eyes. Ace noticed he was awake. "Rise an' shine, soldier," he said. "Day shift'll be over in a little while. That means we work."

Gabe got up, straightening his clothing. "What kind of gear will I need?" he asked Ace.

"Jacket. Gets a little chilly at night."

Not having a jacket, Gabe pulled on the duster. Ace jerked a finger in the direction of Gabe's rifle. "You'll need that, too."

Five minutes later, Gabe was with a party of half a dozen men, walking out the main gate. He hated being on foot, but apparently it was part of the job. Ace seemed to be in charge. He split the men up into two-man groups and sent them off on their rounds. " 'Cause you're new, you stick with me," he told Gabe.

Ace headed toward the mine shaft, Gabe following. A huge gallows frame rose above a large building. Ace led the way into the building. Gabe had seen mines before, but he was impressed by the machinery inside: massive steam engines, huge spools of wire cable, pulleys, smaller engines. Ace walked right up to the edge of the shaft itself, a huge black hole in the ground with cables dangling down into it from the gallows frame.

Gabe heard the clanking of machinery behind him and turned. An operator was engaging the clutch on one of the bigger engines. One of the cables running down into the mine shaft suddenly tightened and began to move. "They're bringing the shift up," Ace told him, shouting over the heavy chuffing of the engine.

Gabe watched the cable rise out of the hole, winding around a huge drum. It rose and rose, but still nothing appeared. Gabe looked over at Ace questioningly. Ace grinned and leaned close to shout into his ear. "It's one hell of a deep hole."

Finally the cage appeared, a huge metal contraption, packed with men. Filthy, tired, bedraggled men. Gabe had seldom seen men who looked so exhausted. Who could have anything to fear from these men? All they would want to do is sleep.

He and Ace watched two more cages packed with men come up. Then the next shift started going down. Gabe thought some of them looked almost as tired as the ones who'd just finished their shift. Ace had already told him that the men worked twelve-hour shifts. He wondered how long a man could last before he was completely worn-out, useless for any more work.

He noticed that, from time to time, the engineer running the lift cage would hit a big lever that actuated a brake, then the cable would stop running for a couple of minutes. "What's he doing?" Gabe asked.

"There's tunnels at different levels," Ace explained. "Gotta let men off at different places."

"How can he tell when the cage reaches a particular level?" Gabe asked.

"There's a dial connected to the cable drum. It tells him when he's gotta put on the brake."

Gabe tried to imagine riding up and down in the cage. The cable moved very fast; the cage must really zoom up and down. If a cable broke . . .

Finally, the entire shift was down. Ace led Gabe on a tour of the building. "Gotta keep an eye on things," he explained. "There's been some sabotage."

"Sounds like the men aren't too happy, then." Gabe said.

Ace shook his head. "Hell no. You seen the men. They got themselves one hell of a rough life. Lots of 'em get killed. More get hurt. Some real bad. One poor bastard lost both his legs. Don't know how he was able to survive. Hell, you couldn't get me to do their kinda work for all the money in the world."

Gabe glanced over at Ace, who was shaking his head. But without real compassion. He was quite willing to ride herd on men he'd just described as living a miserable life. Just as long as he could live a better life.

Gabe felt any possible sympathy for Ace leak away. Ace was the kind of man the mine owners relied on. A man totally for sale.

The night dragged on. Boredom. Gabe heaved a sigh of relief when his shift was over. He and the other men in his guard shift did not get back to the barracks before dawn. Ace and the others fell into bed. Gabe went out to the washhouse, took off his clothes, and poured a bucket of water over himself. He dried off with his shirt, then went back into the bunk room. Snores rose all around. He slipped into his bedroll. The bunk sagged, but he knew he'd sleep. It looked like that would be the shape of his life for a while, sleeping and walking around with a rifle, bored.

Over the next few days, his opinion did not change. Finally, he was freed of night duty at the mine head. Now, he and Ace walked around the company town during the day. "Watch your step near the alleys," Ace warned him. "One of our boys got knifed about a month back."

Gabe did not doubt it. Sometimes he felt he could actually feel the hatred that many of the miners directed at the guards. Or at any company official. Gabe looked for signs of the agitators Jennings had talked about. He saw only workingmen. There was a broad mix of nationalities. Lots of Cornishmen and other Englishmen, with a smattering of Germans and Austrians. There were native-born Americans, too, but they made up less than half the work force. There were also Chinese, but they usually performed the less skilled jobs; many were laundrymen and cooks. "Everybody hates the Chinks," Ace told Gabe. "Jealous, because the Chinks are willing to work like hell for less money. So they take it out on 'em."

One afternoon they came upon several white men beating a Chinese man just inside an alleyway. Another Chinese man hovered several yards away, at the mouth of the alley. Clearly, he wanted to help the man being beaten, but didn't dare. Ace saw what was happening and started to pass on by. Gabe ran into the alley.

"Hey!" Ace shouted after him. "What the hell you think you're doin'? Leave 'em have a little fun."

But Gabe was already inside the alley. "Stop!" he shouted. The men looked around in surprise. No one had ever before tried to stop them from beating up an Oriental. When they saw that it was one of Jennings's guards, their expressions tightened.

"What the hell you buttin' in for?" one bearded man snarled, his accent American. "This ain't none o' your business, scab."

"Why are you beating this man?" Gabe asked, his voice level but his eyes hard.

" 'Cause he's a Chink," the miner replied. "Ain't that enough?"

The Chinese man was lying on the ground, bleeding from the head. The miner drew back his foot and kicked him in the ribs. The man grunted, but was too badly beaten to do more than curl up into a tighter ball.

Gabe felt an instant flash of anger. He'd seen white men beat or kill Indians for the same reason, simply because of their race. He lunged forward and smashed the butt of his rifle into the miner's face. The miner went down, howling around broken teeth. The other four men snarled and started toward Gabe. He cocked the hammer of his Winchester, then pointed it at the belly of the nearest miner.

It was the look in Gabe's eyes, even more than the muzzle of the rifle, that stopped the miners in their tracks. Each man sensed, knew without a doubt, that Gabe would kill them without hesitation. They backed away, then turned and ran from the alley.

Gabe sensed movement from behind him. He spun around, the rifle ready, then saw that it was Ace. "Hey, pardner, take it easy," Ace said, backing away.

Gabe relaxed. He realized now that the long days of boredom had primed him for a fight. This was a bad way to live. He turned toward the injured man, saw that the other Chinese man was now kneeling at his side. Two more Chinese men were cautiously entering the alley.

"Come on," Ace was saying. "Let's get movin' again. There could be trouble now."

Ace walked away. Gabe turned to follow him, but before he did, he saw that all four of the Chinese men, even the injured man, were watching him. One bowed to him, very deeply. Gabe returned a stiff little bow, then left the alley.

When he caught up to Ace, the big man looked over at him with amusement. "You got somethin' goin' for Chinks?" he asked lightly.

"No," Gabe grunted. "But I do like fair fights, and that wasn't a fair fight."

Ace shook his head. "Well, I won't say nothin' about it to Jennings. He'd just get mad. Say you were stirrin' up the miners to no good purpose."

Then Ace scratched his chin. "On the other hand, he might like what you did. Maybe you taught those bastards some respect."

He grinned at Gabe. "Hell, they're gonna be scared shitless o' you now."

CHAPTER SEVEN

Gabe drew special attention from the miners, perhaps because of their initial suspicions about him. When he walked by on patrol, men spat into the mud . . . usually when Gabe was not looking. Ace had been right. His violence against the men beating up the Chinese man had made a lot of people fear him.

Hank was one of the few who openly baited Gabe. The big man with the black beard often muttered when Gabe walked by, and one day had the guts to shout after him, calling Gabe a dirty killer.

One day Gabe ran across Peterson. Gabe walked on by, paying no attention at all to the other man, aware of the surprised look on Peterson's face when he saw Gabe walking patrol with Ace. For a few seconds Gabe wondered if Peterson would be foolish enough to say anything. Of course, if he mentioned the two dead gunmen, Peterson would simply be putting his own head into a noose. To his relief, Peterson simply shook his head sadly and walked away, leaving Gabe uncomfortably aware of the look of deep disappointment on the other man's face.

The days dragged on. Gabe diverted himself by watching Jennings. The more he saw of him, the more complex a man peared to be, not nearly as crude or stupid as Gabe had just believed. For the most part, Jennings kept apart from the men, sitting in his office, drinking; but from time to time, apparently overtaken by manic energy, he would enter the barracks laden with bottles and proceed to lead the men in an orgy of drinking, boasting, and card-playing. When he was in one of these moods, Jennings could drink any of his men under the table. Once, he brought in three prostitutes from the town, who set up shop in the back room. Now Gabe understood what those extra beds were for.

It immediately became apparent to the others that Gabe didn't drink. They shoved bottles at him, but he always declined. Some of the men, drunk, started to become abusive. Until they looked into Gabe's eyes and remembered Ace and the knife. Then they left him alone.

Gabe despised alcohol. He had seen what alcohol had done to his people. He'd seen strong warriors become vomiting, crawling wrecks, once-proud war chiefs sell their wives and daughters for a bottle of cheap trade whiskey, fine women turn into pleading whores. To him, alcohol was the White Man's poison.

There was one other man among the gunmen who didn't drink. A slender, cold man, with the eyes of a killer. His name was Bates. He practiced with his pistol every day. He claimed that he didn't want to drink anything that would slow his reflexes. Bates did not take advantage of any of the whores, either. He was like a monk. A monk of death.

Bates never said much. But he watched Gabe constantly, from across a room, or at the mess hall, whenever he got the chance. Gabe knew Bates was sizing him up. Whatever demons of fear or madness drove Bates had warned him that Gabe was the most dangerous man in the barracks. His demons would eventually demand that he find out who would survive an encounter—himself or Gabe.

Gabe had already been in the fort two weeks when Jennings brought the whores. Gabe sat on his cot, watching, as the men grew more and more drunk. Laughter, shrieks, and moans came from the back room. Some of the men were playing cards. There were low-voiced curses over bad cards, counterpointed by shouts of triumph when a pot was won.

Naturally, among men who lived by the gun, violence was never far beneath the surface. Both the gambling and the women were natural sources of trouble. Which was why Jennings never allowed alcohol or women in the barracks, unless he brought them himself, unless he was there to make certain no trouble started.

This particular night, a fight broke out at one of the card tables. One man was losing heavily. Gabe watched as the man lost hand over hand. Gabe seldom gambled, but he was aware that the man was making some pretty stupid bets. Probably because he was so drunk. Finally, lurching to his feet, his face red with anger and frustration, the loser shouted at one of the men on the far side of the table. "You're cheatin', Jason! An' by God, nobody gets away with cheatin' Pete Soames!"

Jason slowly stood up. "Soames, you fat drunk. I oughta blow a hole right through you."

Both men were very drunk. And both were wearing guns. They backed away from the tables, both hunched over slightly, their right hands drifting toward their pistols. Everyone else scattered, ducking for cover. Once these two drunks started shooting, there was no telling where the bullets might end up.

The only man who did not move was Jennings. He sat at a table a few feet away, with a mostly empty bottle of whiskey in front of him. He picked up his glass and took a sip, watching as the two men squared off. Another second and the lead would start to fly. Finally, Jennings spoke. "Soames . . . Jason . . . go ahead and pull your pieces. But I'm gonna kill whichever one of you gets the other. There ain't gonna be no survivors."

Jennings was sitting behind and to Jason's left. Jason did not dare take his eyes off Soames long enough to turn around and look as Jennings. But Soames shot a glance past Jason. "Aw, boss," he said. "How come you always butt in?"

Jennings lazily took another sip of his whiskey. " 'Cause you eat like a horse, Soames. I got a fortune tied up in you, countin' just the food. I can't afford to lose that investment. Now both o' you . . . back off."

Soames was suddenly looking indecisive. But not Jason. "I can't let it pass, Jennings," he said tightly, still glaring directly at Soames. "He called me a card cheat."

Still seated, Jennings said, "You'll let it pass, Jason. Just 'cause I'm telling you to let it pass."

"Goddamn it, Jennings!" Jason snarled. "You butt in too damned much. This fat asshole . . ."

The scrape of chair legs against the floor as Jennings stood up finally forced Jason to face away from Soames; there was now a much greater danger behind him. Jason turned around, and as he turned, Jennings drew. It was one of the fastest draws Gabe had ever seen, a movement so smooth that one moment Jennings's right hand was by his side, the next moment it was a foot from Jason's face, with a pistol growing out of his fist, the hammer already cocked back.

The room had now fallen into a dead silence. Jason stood frozen in place, his pistol still in its holster, his hand a foot away from its butt. "You're kinda skinny, Jason," Jennings said, his voice cold, and now totally sober. "There's not all that much invested in you, not in food, anyhow, not like Soames. Not so's I'd mind investing two hundred and forty grains o' lead right up your goddamned nose."

Jason stared down at Jennings's pistol. The muzzle was so close that his eyes had to cross so that he could see it. "Okay. Okay, boss. But how can I just let it pass? He called me a . . ."

"Oh, I'm sure Soames will take it back," Jennings said. He flicked a glance over at Soames, then right back to Jason. "Isn't that right, Soames?"

Before Soames could answer, Jennings added, "And you, Jason. You'll take back calling Soames fat."

That broke the tension. Some of the men laughed; Soames did have a considerable paunch. Jason backed away a step, careful to keep his hand away from his gun. "Hell," he said, managing a smile. "I think I'll just start callin' old Soames 'Bones.' "

Jennings, pistol still in hand, turned toward Soames. "How about it, Bones?"

Soames struggled with anger for a moment, then shrugged, his hands held well away from his body, palms up. "What the hell? Guess I got a little hot under the collar."

That was obviously as close as either man would get to an apology. But the moment had passed, the tension was defused. Jennings's pistol disappeared back into its holster as smoothly as it had come out. Soames immediately went over to his bunk and lay down. He was almost immediately asleep. Passed out, Gabe figured.

Jason was still standing in place, perhaps trying to figure out how much he'd been made to look like a fool. Then he abruptly turned and headed for the back room. Some unlucky whore was in for a rough ride.

Jennings watched them both go. But Gabe was watching Bates, who was staring intently at Jennings's back. He's wondering if he can take him, Gabe thought.

Jennings sat down. He looked up, straight at Gabe. A little smile flickered over his lips. He stood up again. "Conrad . . . come with me."

He led the way outside. Gabe was happy enough to go; the noise in the room was beginning to bother him.

Jennings was standing near one of the hitching racks. He spoke, without turning around. "Well . . . that's how you handle assholes like that."

He turned to face Gabe. "You know that, and I know that, but as for the rest of those cattle . . ."

He looked straight into Gabe's face, as if searching for something. For just a moment there was a hint of vulnerability in Jennings's expression. Then—perhaps he did not see what he was looking for—his expression went blank again. Blank and cold. "Go back inside, Conrad. Get laid. Do something human, for God's sake."

Gabe watched him go. There was just a slight slouch to Jennings's shoulders. He'd wanted something from Gabe, wanted to share something. But to Gabe, there was nothing to share. A man who chose fighting as a way of life he could understand. But a man who sold his fighting ability for money was not a man he could call friend.

All that talk Jennings had spouted, about the union men being foreign agitators, Reds, maybe they were, maybe they weren't, what mattered to Gabe was the undeniable fact that Jennings had sold his gun to wealthy thieves. Maybe that was what was bothering Jennings. Maybe that was why he drank, why he pushed his luck to the limit. He was an impressive man in some ways, but definitely a fallen man, a corrupted warrior.

One night Gabe saw Joe, the informer, come slinking into the fort. Jennings took him into the office. Half an hour later, after Joe had left, Jennings called Ace and another man into the office. Before he closed the door, Jennings noticed Gabe, standing a few yards away. He hesitated, as if he were about to invite Gabe inside with the other two men, but then he walked back inside and closed the door.

Gabe quickly walked toward the dark shadows behind the office. There was a window there, and since it was a warm night, the window was open. Gabe felt uncomfortable eavesdropping, but he knew something was about to happen, and instinct told him to find out what it was.

"So," he heard Jennings say to Ace and the other man, "how are things in town and around the mine?"

Ace's voice replied, "Not too good, boss. Tension's risin'. We don't seem to scare 'em too much anymore."

"Yeah," Jennings replied. "That's what I just heard from another source. There's talk of a strike."

"Yeah, yeah. We kinda got that impression, too. Heard some rough talk. There's rabble-rousers shootin' off their mouths. Like that bastard, Hank. He's always rantin' and ravin' about somethin'. An' a lot of the miners are startin' to listen."

"Maybe we oughta do somethin' about this Hank," the other man cut in. Gabe remembered his name as Buck. "See that he . . . has a little accident?"

"No," Jennings replied. "Hank's got a big mouth, but he's not all that dangerous. If those idiots start following a shithead like Hank, we're home free. It's the others we have to worry about. Like Peterson."

A small silence followed. "Peterson?" Ace said. "He don't seem to say much."

"He's not a talker," Jennings said. "He's a doer. A planner. A report I just got says that it's Peterson who's actually setting things up. Forming a strike committee, just like those Reds do over in Europe. He makes plans, he knows the law. He's more dangerous than a hundred Hanks."

Jennings's voice dropped a little, became thoughtful. "Remember those two yahoos we sent out after Peterson? The two who never came back? We figured, because there wasn't any big blowup, that they'd just decided to keep on ridin', never got near Peterson at all. Now, I'm not so sure. Maybe Peterson took care of them."

"Peterson?" Ace scoffed. "He ain't no fighter."

"That's right. Like I said, he's a thinker. Maybe he sucked 'em into a trap. Got help gettin' rid of 'em."

"Hmm." Ace's voice. "That makes more sense, I s'pose. They were good boys, not the kind who'd just ride on off. Jeez . . . I never figured Peterson for a dangerous man."

"Well, I'm starting to," Jennings said. "And I figure we gotta get rid of him. That's why I called you and Buck in here."

"Yeah? Well, hell, boss, that might not be so easy. He hangs around with that bunch over at that old house. They're pretty heavily armed. If just the two of us—"

Jennings out him off. "I didn't call you in here to commit suicide. I happen to know that Peterson will be alone for a while tonight. And I know where he'll be. So it'll be just you two and him."

There was a mutter of approval, then Jennings continued. "There's a meeting of a strike committee. Real secret, of course, 'cause they know we don't let 'em meet openly. Which means that the members of that committee go there alone, one by one. And leave the same way."

Gabe listened as Jennings told Ace and Buck where the meeting was being held. There was only one route Peterson could take to get home. "Great," Ace said, obviously pleased with what was expected of him. "We'll fill him so fulla holes—"

"Uh-uh," Jennings cut in. "Nothing that simple. I want you to grab him alive. That shouldn't be hard. I've never seen him carrying a gun. Then take him over behind the shaft building and hang him from one of the gantries. So they'll find him there in the morning. That'll put the fear of God into the rest of 'em a hell of a lot better than gunfire."

Gabe heard more mutters of approval from Ace and Buck. A moment later, the meeting was over. Gabe backed away from the window as the front door opened. A few more words, which Gabe couldn't hear, were exchanged, and then Ace and Buck headed toward the main gate.

Still keeping to the shadows, Gabe entered the stables. It was dark inside, but there was enough light spilling from neighboring windows to let him find a long coil of rope.

He took the rope outside, behind the stables. The back wall of the stables butted right up against the log palisade at the rear of the fort. It was easy to climb onto the stable roof, then hoist himself up onto the top of the palisade. A guard passed this spot every few minutes, but had to cut around the stable. Gabe had noticed that the guards seldom looked up; too dark to see much here, anyway. Gabe had long ago marked this area as a way out, if he ever needed one.

The hard part would be getting back in; there was a twelve-foot drop on the far side. That was where the rope came in. Gabe looped the center of the rope around the top of one of the palisade's logs, then dropped the loose ends over the side, down toward the ground. A moment later he had slid down the rope and was standing in darkness behind the fort. He'd have to leave the rope here so he could climb back in and hope that no one noticed it. He doubted they would, not before morning.

Moving silently in his moccasins, Gabe melted away into the darkness. He, too, was aware of the route Peterson would have to take coming back from his meeting. He reached the area a few minutes later. Now, he would have to find Ace and Buck.

It took him another ten minutes. Both men were poor at ambush, at least compared to an Oglala. Buck coughed once. Then Gabe heard Ace scratching himself; the sound of fingernails against denim was surprisingly loud in the quiet night air.

Buck was closest, about forty yards away, hidden behind a shed, while Ace was another thirty yards further along, in a thick clump of brush.

Buck would be the most difficult to stalk; the ground leading up to his position was mostly open. But Gabe was an expert at stalking. Moving with infinite care, trying to merge with every tiny bit of cover, appearing as just another shadow among shadows, he slowly moved in on Buck. Within ten minutes, he was only six feet away. But a long six feet, all of it open ground between buildings. And Buck was apparently ill at ease; he kept looking around him nervously. Gabe doubted he could reach the man silently, without being seen first.

And silence was of the utmost importance. He did not wish to kill either Buck or Ace, and if there was a struggle with Buck, Ace would come running, and there would be a gunfight. The whole area would be alerted.

Gabe bent slowly, picked up a small stone. Very carefully, making certain there was no rustle of clothing, no rasping of the stone against his fingernails as he threw, he lobbed the stone over Buck's head. The stone landed a few feet in front of Buck. The direction Peterson should be coming from.

Buck leaned forward, craning his neck, all his attention focused toward the street. Gabe was on him in an instant, his pistol out, lashing forward, cracking against Buck's head. Buck grunted, went down. By now Gabe's free hand was over

Buck's mouth, muffling any more groans. He eased Buck's limp body to the ground and dragged him further behind the shack. Pulling some piggin' string from his pocket—something else he'd picked up in the stable—he quickly lashed Buck's hands behind him, tied his ankles together, then stuffed his bandanna into his mouth. Buck was still unconscious when Gabe dumped him into the shed.

Now, Ace. Gabe slipped around behind the shed and began his approach toward the brush where Ace was concealed. Or thought he was concealed. It took another ten minutes, but finally Gabe was less than a yard away from the big man, completely blended in with the brush, waiting for his chance.

Ace was clearly growing bored. He kept changing his position. "Come on . . . come on, you son of a bitch," he muttered.

Gabe moved forward another few inches. In just a few seconds . . .

Then Ace suddenly stiffened. He stared to his left for a moment, then swiveled his head toward his right, the direction where Buck had been waiting. "Hey!" Ace hissed. "It's Peterson! Here he comes!"

Damn! Gabe thought. If Peterson had held off for just another couple of minutes . . .

Gabe had no choice but to act now. Ace might leave the bushes at any moment, rush out at Peterson. He was on his knees already, tensed, ready to move.

Gabe leapt on Ace from behind, circled his right arm around the man's neck, then grabbed hold of his own left forearm, while his left hand pressed hard against the back of Ace's head.

Ace reacted instinctively, clawing at the arm around his throat. A bad decision. Gabe's hold tightened, shutting off Ace's air. And the blood to his brain. Too late Ace groped for the pistol on his hip, but by now Gabe had locked his legs around Ace's body, pinning the pistol in place.

It was all over quickly. Ace struggled wildly, and he was strong, but with no blood getting past the choke hold, he began to black out. A few more frantic jerks, and he suddenly slumped. Gabe kept up the pressure for another few seconds, trying to gauge at what point it would ensure unconsciousness, and at what point kill Ace.

He discovered he now had another problem. Peterson, hearing Gabe and Ace thrashing around in the brush, had come running over. "What the hell . . ." Peterson started to say.

By now Gabe had released the pressure. Ace slumped down, out like a light. "Shh," Gabe hissed. "They were going to kill you."

Now Peterson realized who Gabe was. "You!" he said sharply.

"Shut up!" Gabe repeated. He didn't want his name mentioned. Just in case Buck might have regained consciousness. Gabe stood up. Peterson recoiled away from him. Speaking quietly and rapidly, Gabe explained what had happened.

While Peterson mulled it over, Gabe bent down and quickly tied and gagged Ace, as he had Buck. With both men secured, he guided Peterson far enough away so that they could not be overheard. Peterson looked at him for a long time. "What kind of game are you playing?" he finally asked.

Gabe shrugged. "I don't know. But I couldn't just stand by and let them kill you. Not after all the trouble I went to before. With those other two."

Peterson, reminded of how much he already owed Gabe, relaxed a little. "You're working for us then?"

Gabe shook his head emphatically. "I don't work for anybody. I do what I feel like doing. Maybe I'll be moving on soon, but there are some things you should know."

He told Peterson about Joe, the informer. Peterson seemed shocked. "That's terrible! I thought he was with us all the way."

"I suppose you'll kill him then."

Peterson shook his head. "It's a temptation. But maybe, now that we know, we should just go on pretending we know nothing. We can feed him phony information."

Peterson shook his head disgustedly. "Goddamn, but I hate this kind of thing!"

His words made Gabe feel he'd done the right thing, helped the right man. He quickly told Peterson where he'd left Buck and suggested what he might do with Buck and Ace. Even in the dark, he could see Peterson beginning to smile. Peterson was no killer, and Gabe had left him a way to avoid killing.

Gabe left before Peterson could thank him again. He made it back to the fort with no trouble, used the rope to scale the wall, then dropped down onto the stable roof. No challenges, apparently no one had seen him. To play it safe, he made sure as many men as possible noticed him that night. Particularly the gate guards, who would remember that he had not left the fort, or at any rate, not gone past them.

When he went to bed that night, Gabe had trouble getting to sleep. Partly because of the excitement of the past hour. Partly because of something Peterson had asked him. A good question. What the hell kind of game *was* he playing?

CHAPTER EIGHT

The next morning, just as it grew light, while the morning shift was shuffling toward the mine shaft, Ace and Buck were found dangling from a gantry near the mine entrance, trussed up like chickens, blindfolded and gagged, hanging from ropes tied around their torsos. Pinned to the front of each man's shirt was a placard reading "Assassin."

Jennings was furious. He had been up late the night before, drinking. Now, his mind still foggy, he was drinking again, as Ace and Buck stood in front of him in his office. Buck, still dizzy from the clout on his head, was having trouble standing. Ace stood motionless, his face expressionless as he listened to Jennings scream at him. "And you didn't see anything? Anything at all?" Jennings demanded.

"I told ya, boss, I was blindfolded when I came to," Ace replied sourly.

"Yeah," Buck added. He tried shaking his aching head and nearly fell. He had a slight concussion. "Same with me."

Jennings glared at Buck, then turned back toward Ace. "You said somebody grabbed you, choked you?"

"Yeah. Just as Peterson showed up. It hadda be some kind of setup. Peterson got my attention, then they snuck up from behind and jumped me."

"They?"

"Yeah. Hadda be more than one of 'em. They were all over me."

Jennings fumed for a while. "It was a setup, then. We were sold out. We got a spy among us."

He stood up, started toward the door, then stopped long enough to pick up a bottle of whiskey. Drinking directly out of the bottle, he took a hefty slug, slammed the bottle back down onto the table, then stalked out of his office toward the gate. The gate guards, knowing Jennings was in a bad mood, stiffened into attitudes of alertness as he approached.

"Who was on duty last night?" Jennings demanded.

"Which shift?" one guard asked.

Then Jennings remembered that he had set up two night shifts, so that the guards would not grow tired and therefore careless. "Think, shithead," Jennings snarled. "About ten last night."

The guard's face darkened with anger. Jennings reflected for a moment that these were not men to insult; he had purposely picked some real hard cases. But his anger came crashing back, intensified by his hangover.

"Jones and Thompson," the guard said sullenly. He wanted to tell Jennings to go to hell, but he was afraid of him. Still, if he called him a name again . . .

But Jennings was already striding away. He slammed open the door of the barracks. Men sat up, blinking. Some reached for the guns that were always close by their beds, then saw that it was their boss. Jennings walked over to a bunk. "Jones," he snapped. "Who went out last night? Around ten."

Jones was still blinking sleep from his eyes. Propped up on his elbows, holes showing in his dirty long johns, he shook his head to clear it. "Last night?" he murmured. "Ten o'clock? Well . . . just Ace. Ace and Buck. That's all I remember."

"No, damn it! Before Ace and Buck. Within a half hour before they left."

Jones was fully awake now. In his profession, waking up too slowly could be fatal. "Just that miner. The one who comes and sees you once in a while. I don't know his name."

"Joe," Jennings said under his breath. "If that son of a bitch is selling me out . . .

"No one else? No one else went out the gate?" he asked Jones.

Jones shook his head. "Not a single man, boss."

Jennings nodded curtly, then turned around and stalked out of the barracks. He walked up to one of the inner-perimeter guards. "Get on over to the mine," he snapped. "Pick up a couple of men in town. Bring me Joe Williams."

Ten minutes later, Gabe, patrolling alone since Ace had not shown up for duty, was approached by the guard. "Boss's orders," the man said. "I'm going down into the mine. Bringing a man back up. You stay topside and watch the shaft."

The guard led the way to the shaft head. Once inside the big building, Gabe watched as the man stepped into the cage, signaled to the lift man, then disappeared down into the shaft.

Gabe smiled. Peterson had done a good job. As far as Gabe was concerned, it would have been all right if Peterson had hanged Ace and Buck by their necks. But this way was better. Better to humiliate Jennings and his men. And scare them a little, because Ace and Buck could just as easily be dead. Up until now there had been little violence against the guards, except for the one who'd been stabbed some time ago. Most of the violence had traveled in the other direction. Now, maybe Jennings and his men would walk just a little more nervously. Maybe some would quit. As Gabe intended to do. He was tired of this game. He'd seen what he wanted to see, it was time to move on.

He was surprised when the other guard reappeared at the head of the shaft, towing the spy named Joe. "You come along," he told Gabe. "Had a little trouble down there. Had to pull my gun."

Indeed, more men had formed up around the shaft head. "Hey, what's goin' on?" one man called out. "How come those scabs are takin' Joe outta here?"

There was more muttering among the men. The guard who'd brought Joe up from below looked nervous. The audacity of what had been done to Ace and Buck was enough to make all of the guards nervous. "Let's get the hell outta here," the guard muttered.

They shoved Joe out the door. "Hey! What'd I do?" Joe whined, but went along docilely enough.

Gabe wondered what might have happened if there'd been more men on the street. But with one shift down the hole, and the other mostly asleep, they made it to the fort without difficulty. What crazy idea, Gabe wondered, was going through Jennings's mind, to bring his spy openly to the fort? The miners would wonder, too. Joe would be compromised. He could end up useless to Jennings in the future.

When they reached the fort, Jennings stormed out of his office, very drunk. For once out-of-control drunk, and his drunkenness had obviously clouded his judgment. In front of all the men, he walked up to Joe, grabbed him by the front of his shirt, and screamed in his face, "You goddamn little pig! You sold us out!"

Joe's face was as white as a sheet. "What the hell are you talkin' about?" he bleated.

Jennings's face was ugly. Gabe wondered if he might shoot Joe. "You tipped off Peterson," Jennings said, his voice lower now and very cold. "You tipped him off about Ace and Buck."

"Tipped him?" Joe spluttered. "But how could I? I didn't know nothin' about Ace and Buck! I didn't know anybody was gonna jump two of your boys!"

Then realization hit Jennings. Of course. He hadn't even decided to send Ace and Buck to nail Peterson until after Joe had left the fort. There was no way Joe could have known. He shoved Joe away from him. "Get him the hell outta here," he snarled. He glared at Gabe and at the other guard, the one he'd sent after Joe. He started to turn away, to head back toward his office, but he stopped himself and turned back to face Gabe. He continued to stare at Gabe for several seconds, trying to remember something about him. An image of Gabe. . . . But it wouldn't come to him.

Jennings's mind was spinning, overtaxed by a combination of whiskey, rage, and humiliation. He was beginning to realize how stupid it had been to bring Joe here in broad daylight, under guard. Peterson would be smart enough to become suspicious of Joe. They'd grab him, make him talk. Probably kill him. Well, that was Joe's problem now. Jennings stormed into his office, slammed the door behind him, and reached for the whiskey.

A mood of sullen anger now settled over the fort. Each man felt humiliated by Ace and Buck's humiliation. Before the next guard shift came on duty, Jennings, sober now, or as sober as he ever got, came into the barracks and addressed the men. "Watch your asses out there. Those shitheads are gonna be feelin' big now. Don't take any shit off 'em."

For the next couple of days, guards and miners sullenly watched one another. There was a report that Joe had been ridden out of town on a rail, tarred and feathered. Peterson, who pretty much kept out of sight, was surrounded by armed men. Jennings began mumbling about maybe having to wire back East for more guards.

The company gunmen now patrolled in groups of three or four. One afternoon Gabe was out patrolling with Buck and with Bates, the slender killer. Gabe noticed that there were more miners than usual on the company town's muddy streets. Apparently some of the men were not going below to work their shifts.

The mood was ugly. Most of the miners stared at the gunmen with open hostility. Some of the miners, now that they'd seen Ace and Buck humiliated, were beginning to think of the guards as paper tigers, starting to hold them in contempt. Gabe knew how dangerous an attitude that was. There was not a man in the barracks who was not a killer at heart. Peterson should have foreseen that. Of course, maybe he had. Maybe he was looking for a confrontation.

One was on the way. Some of the miners recognized Buck

as one of the men who'd been trussed up on the gantry. Hoots and jeers followed him down the street. By the time the little group of three had reached the end of the street, Buck was seething. The three guards turned around and started back. One of the miners, obviously drunk, stepped out into Buck's path. The miner was a big man. He grinned, breathing out whiskey fumes. "Been doin' any high flyin' lately?" he asked.

Gabe could see Buck tensing, his right hand drifting toward his gun butt. "Take it easy," Gabe warned him. "Jennings said we weren't supposed to . . ."

But it was too late. Several other miners, standing nearby, guffawed loudly. The big miner was still talking. "We don't need your kind around these parts, yella belly," he snarled. "Get the hell outta here before we . . ."

Cursing, Buck stepped forward. His fist lashed out, knocking the miner to the ground. Buck fumbled for his pistol and pulled it out of its holster. He was cocking the hammer when Gabe stepped in and grabbed the pistol, slipping his thumb beneath the hammer so it couldn't fall. "Not when he's down," Gabe snapped. "It'd be murder, then there'd be trouble."

"Get the hell away from me, you half-breed freak," Buck snarled. That angered Gabe. He twisted the pistol away from Buck with his left hand, while he slammed the bottom of his right fist against Buck's jaw.

Buck fell. There were shouts from the watching miners. Gabe started to turn toward the miners, until he heard a voice calling out from behind him. Bates's voice, cool, deadly, gloating. "Conrad," Bates said. "Buck was right. You're a goddamn Injun-loving freak. And you just made a big mistake, turnin' against us."

Gabe turned around slowly. Bates was standing about fifteen feet away, legs braced, with his right hand held a bit out to the side, near the butt of his pistol. "It's time, Conrad," Bates said. "Time we settled it out between us."

Gabe looked quickly over toward Buck, who was shaking

his head, about ready to get up. He did not look happy. Gabe tossed Buck's pistol out into the street, where it sank into the mud. But even unarmed, Buck was off to his right, Bates to his left. He would not be able to watch both men at the same time.

Bates came to the same conclusion. "Buck!" he snapped. "I want you to stay out of this. It's between me and Conrad."

Buck was getting to his feet, glaring at Gabe. "The hell you say," he snarled. "I want a piece o' the bastard's hide."

"No!" Bates snapped. "You stay out of this, or by God, I'll put my first bullet into you!"

Buck shrugged and stepped back. "Okay, Bates. But if you miss, he's mine."

Now Bates smiled. "Oh, I won't miss. Mr. Conrad is gonna get a bellyful of lead."

His eyes locked onto Gabe's. "Go ahead and make your move, Conrad. That is, if you've got the guts. But if you don't make that move real soon, then I'll gun you down where you stand."

Freed of worrying about Buck, Gabe focused all his attention on Bates. He recognized a kind of nervous glee in the other man's eyes. A murderous excitement. He read other things there, too. Calculation. He saw Bates's eyes focus for a brief instant on Gabe's broken trigger finger, then dart toward his left hand. He knew what Bates was thinking; that he would have to draw with his left. Both of Gabe's pistols were worn in a manner that would indicate he intended to draw with his left. It was a warm day; Gabe was not wearing his duster. The gun on his right hip, worn butt forward, and the gun in the shoulder hoister beneath his right armpit were both clearly visible.

Gabe had seen Bates shoot. He knew he was both fast and accurate. A very dangerous opponent. Gabe was going to have to use his head if he wanted to walk away alive.

A silence had fallen over the street. All eyes were on the two combatants. Gabe settled his body. He noticed that Bates was still watching his left hand, a stupid thing to do; he should have been watching Gabe's entire body. Gabe moved his left hand ever so slightly closer to his shoulder rig and saw Bates smile, a quick jerking of his lips, his body tensing as he got ready to draw.

Then apparently losing courage, Gabe let his left hand drift away from the shoulder holster. Bates's eyes followed that hand, not realizing that by now Gabe's right hand was practically on the butt of the pistol at his hip. Gabe saw some of the tension leave Bates's body. "You yellow . . ." Bates started to say.

By then Gabe was drawing with his right, a somewhat clumsy move, with the butt of the pistol on his right hip pointing forward, but the move took Bates completely by surprise. By the time Bates reacted, it was too late. Bates clawed for his gun with incredible speed, but the move was just a trifle too rushed.

Gabe already had his pistol out and pointed at Bates. Gabe didn't try to aim, there was no time for that. Instead, holding the trigger back with the bent tip of his right finger, he slammed the heel of his left hand against the hammer spur, fanning the hammer back, not once, but three times, the three shots following one another so closely that they sounded like one continuous roar.

One of the bullets missed. One hit Bates in the ribs, spinning him partly around; the other took him in the throat. Bates staggered backward. He managed to fire his pistol once, but harmlessly, up at the sky. His left hand clawed at his throat; he was clearly choking on his own blood. Desperately, fighting pain and panic, he managed to lower his gun hand, trying to aim at Gabe, who, now that he had plenty of time, cocked his pistol and put a bullet right through the center of Bates's chest.

Bates flew backward, landing flat in the mud, his pistol falling from his hand. Gabe immediately spun around, looking for trouble behind him. Nothing. Buck, unarmed, was staring at Bates. The miners, wide-eyed, were too frightened to move.

Gabe turned back toward Bates. The slender gunman's legs jerked a few times, then he lay still.

Gabe immediately shucked the four empties from his pistol and punched four fresh rounds into the cylinder. He'd already heard it, the fort's gates crashing open, the sound of running feet pounding in his direction. He thought of getting the hell away from there, but his horse was at the fort, along with his rifles. He wouldn't get far on foot. He doubted the miners would help him.

And then it was too late. Half a dozen men, four with rifles, two with shotguns, were running toward him. Ace was leading the pack. He was not looking particularly friendly.

CHAPTER NINE

The walk back to the fort was tense. Gabe was up front, with Ace to one side. Four men further back carried Bates's dead body. Ace had decided to get Bates off the street quickly, before the miners got used to looking at a dead guard, and got ideas.

Jennings was waiting just outside his office. "What the hell happened?" he demanded of both Ace and Gabe.

Ace jerked a thumb toward Buck. "Says Conrad shot Bates."

Jennings turned cold eyes on Gabe. "That right?"

Gabe shrugged. "It was Bates's idea. He claimed it was time we figured out who was the better man."

"Huh," Jennings snorted. "That does sound like Bates, all right."

"Hey, boss," Buck cut in. "It wasn't like that. Conrad here, he decked me 'cause o' some miner, then Bates, he stepped right in. Shit, if Conrad hadn't o' suckered Bates, he'd o' been the one layin'—"

"You'll get your chance to talk, Buck . . . starting now," Jennings said in a bored voice. But his eyes were not bored. They remained alert as he patiently worked the story out of Buck, about the miner with the big mouth, the fact that

Buck was about to shoot that miner when Gabe grabbed his pistol.

"And just why did you do that?" Jennings asked, turning to face Gabe.

Gabe met Jennings's eyes. "You said we weren't supposed to take any crap. But you also said to be careful not to touch off any incidents. I figured that shooting an unarmed man, while he was lying on his back, would have been one hell of an incident."

Jennings nodded. "Yeah. There might be something in what you say." Then his eyes narrowed. "You make it all sound so logical, Conrad. But there's something about you, some little thing that bothers me. You ain't really one of us, are you? And then there's . . ."

Jennings's eyes narrowed even further. "I just remembered something," he murmured. "Something that was bothering me the other day. Something that was layin' at the back of my mind. And now it's all startin' to come back to me. I saw you. That night Ace and Buck got waylaid. You were standing near the office when I called them inside. You looked real interested. You looked like you wanted to know what was goin' on. I nearly called you in with them. . . ."

Gabe remained silent, trying to look confused, like he didn't know what Jennings was talking about.

"Could it be?" Jennings said, his voice deceptively mild. "Were you the one who tipped off Peterson? Maybe you even . . . But the guards said nobody left the fort."

Jennings eyes were boring into Gabe's. Gabe knew he had no real facts to go on, but men like Jennings didn't need facts. Suspicions were enough. Ace had not taken Gabe's guns. Gabe wondered if he should go for his pistol now, try to take Jennings out before the others cut him down. Several men had gathered around, looking for something, anything that would alleviate the normal boredom. Gabe turned his head slightly. He noticed that Ace, his eyes nearly as suspicious as Jennings's, had the muzzle of his shotgun more or less trained on him. No, he'd never clear leather before Ace blasted him.

"Conrad," Jennings was saying. "I can't prove it, but there's something rotten here. And in a situation like this, we don't take chances."

Gabe decided he would go for it only if Jennings went for his own gun. He was becoming more and more certain that Jennings was thinking about shooting him.

"But," Jennings continued, "I don't want to go flyin' off half-cocked. We gotta have justice around here. Fair play."

Justice? Gabe thought. Among these hired mercenaries?

"So I'll tell you what I'm gonna do. I ain't gonna kill you, Conrad. Not yet, anyhow. But I can't let you run around loose, either."

Jennings jerked his head toward a couple of the men. "Get his guns," he snapped.

Gabe thought once again of going for it, of trying to fight his way out. But he realized that course of action would mean certain death, even if he took Jennings and a couple of the others with him. No point in fighting, anyhow. It sounded as if Jennings was going to lock him up. Fine, let him. There was no real guardhouse in this jury-rigged fort. Nothing he couldn't bust out of.

But Jennings had other ideas. As the men stripped Gabe of his weapons, Jennings said, "When you first showed up, Conrad, I offered you a job. I wouldn't want to go back on my word. Besides, we don't let people mooch around here. So, until I make up my mind about you, I'm just gonna change your job a little."

Jennings smiled. He looked pleased with himself. "So . . . you go down the mine with the next shift. You're gonna start earnin' an honest livin', Conrad."

It was late afternoon when they took Gabe to the pithead. He was flanked by several gunmen, so there wasn't much point in trying anything. He looked around him as they proceeded down the town's main street. Some of the miners were watching him with curiosity. Some even looked sympathetic. Word had probably gotten around about him saving the big miner from Buck's bullet. Also, they must have noticed that he'd been disarmed.

Gabe was led into the big building over the pithead. He glanced at the mine shaft itself—a big, ragged, black hole in the ground.

Ace, whom Jennings had entrusted with this detail, beckoned a man over toward him. "New man," Ace said, jerking his head in Gabe's direction. "You help him get broke in."

The man came over to Gabe. "You ever worked in a mine before?" he asked.

Gabe shook his head. The man smiled. A humorless smile. "Well then . . . you got a lot of fun ahead."

Gabe said nothing. The man didn't appear to be hostile; he was just some kind of minor boss, one who knew which side of his bread held the butter.

Men were beginning to form up for the next shift. All were waiting for the cage to come up from below, bringing the men from the previous shift. The man Ace had called over remained near Gabe. Gabe was looking over at the huge steam engines. He'd never really paid much attention to the equipment before, but now it looked as if he was going to have a much more intimate acquaintance with the way the mine worked.

The man—Gabe had by now heard him described as the top-landers' boss—noticed that Gabe was looking at one of the engines in particular. It was enormous. Its flywheel was easily ten feet in diameter. And it was turning. Gabe had never been here when that flywheel was not turning. "It's a pump," the top-landers' boss said, cutting into Gabe's thoughts. "Real wet down there. Gotta keep ahead of it. We pump out hundreds of thousands of gallons a day."

The man seemed about to continue, but his eyes lit on something behind Gabe. "Ah," he said. "There's Heerden. He'll take you in hand, get you used to the way we do things."

Gabe turned. A big man had just come into the building. He'd noticed him several times before, had been told he was a foreman. From the first time he'd seen him, Gabe had sensed an air of casual brutality about the man, a brutality that seemed to fit right in with this particular mining operation.

Ace waved the foreman over. Gabe noticed that Heerden looked straight at Ace with no fear at all evident in his eyes. Those eyes were small and bright, buried behind bone and leathery skin.

"Got one for you," Ace said, jerking his thumb toward Gabe. "Special case. Jennings said to keep an eye on him."

Heerden looked Gabe over. His lips curled into a slight sneer. "I don't think I'll have any trouble with this one."

Heerden spoke with a guttural foreign accent, which Gabe could not quite place. Heerden came closer and stood right in front of him, his face only inches from Gabe's, exhaling whiskey fumes.

Heerden was not only big, but he gave off a feeling of brute strength, animal power. His shoulders and chest were massive, his forearms knotted with muscle. A rock-like head was set upon his thick neck. His face was devoid of anything that might be described as compassion.

Gabe said nothing. Heerden waited for a moment, then suddenly, with no warning, no windup, sank a short punch into Gabe's stomach, knocking the wind out of him. He gasped and started to bend forward, then stopped the movement and straightened up, not letting his eyes stray from Heerden's.

Heerden met Gabe's cold gaze easily. He actually smiled. Just a little. A smile of anticipated pleasure. "You bring me tough one this time," he said to Ace.

Then all his attention refocused onto Gabe. "You listen to me, tough man. My name is Piet Heerden. I am from South Africa, where we have mines that make this one look like gopher hole. In this hole—how you say here? Ya . . . your ass belong to me. You screw up, you don't see daylight again. I don't like all this—how is it said? Pussyfooting. Back home, we know how to do it. We have black men who do the work, kaffirs. And we know how to work with kaffirs. We have this big whip made of hippo hide. One blow takes the skin off a man, breaks bones. You give me trouble, I take your hide off with my bare hands."

By now, the cage had come up. Miners from the previous shift were stumbling wearily from the cage. Heerden prodded Gabe toward the cage. "We go below now. You get to see hell, up close."

As they walked onto the swaying floor of the cage, Heerden laughed. "And me?" he said, poking his thumb into his own chest. "You're gonna find out. Me . . . I'm the Devil himself."

CHAPTER TEN

The cage filled with men. Gabe was crowded toward the back. Heerden stayed near him. Suddenly the floor seemed to drop away from under them. Gabe instinctively grabbed hold of one of the wooden slats, and now he and the other men were in partial darkness, descending at an incredible rate of speed. He turned. Heerden was grinning at him. "We go fast, no? Maybe t'ousand feet a minute."

When Gabe wrapped an arm around one of the cage supports, Heerden pulled him away. "You let your arm hang out, you lose it," he snapped.

Then Gabe became aware of how fast the shaft was whizzing by, outside the cage. Just a blur of rock, briefly lit by the glare of lamps from inside the cage; an occasional glimpse of a lit tunnel, there for an instant, then gone again.

A thousand feet a minute? Then why were they still falling? Could the mine really be so deep?

And still the cage plunged downward. Gabe noticed that it was growing hotter. Suddenly the cage jerked to a stop, right at the mouth of a tunnel. Some of the men got off. Gabe started to follow, but Heerden pulled him back. "Not yet," the South African said. "You go all the way down."

The cage dropped again. Another interminable time of falling. Finally, the cage jerked to a stop, then hung, bouncing
slightly on its long cable. The last of the men were getting off.
Heerden jerked his chin at Gabe. Gabe got off, too. Heerden
handed him a lamp. Gabe had already noticed that all the men
were carrying lamps.

Gabe's eyes were getting used to the dim light. He saw
that they were in a large cavern. Big open boxes made of
heavy timbers reached up to the cavern's roof. Heerden led
the way through aisles between the boxes. At the cavern's far
end, Gabe saw the narrow mouth of a tunnel, gaping against
rock. Heerden entered the tunnel. Gabe followed.

With rock above him, Gabe instinctively ducked, until he
noticed that Heerden, who was about the same height as
himself, was walking erect, his head clearing the rock by
several inches. So Gabe straightened up, too.

Finally, they reached the end of the tunnel. Several miners
were standing, talking. "You get to work!" Heerden snarled.
"Or, by God, I make you hurt!"

A couple of the men stared back at Heerden. Gabe saw the
anger in their eyes mixed with hatred. But, after a slight pause,
perhaps just to show they were not to be pushed around, they
turned and began picking up tools.

Heerden tapped one of the men on the shoulder. "Taffy,"
he said. "This is a new man. I want you to make sure he
doesn't get killed his first day. He'll be mucking out."

With that, Heerden simply turned and walked away. The
man he'd called Taffy looked after him until Heerden and his
lamp had faded away into the tunnel's blackness. Judging from
Taffy's expression, Gabe suspected that he did not particularly
like Heerden. But then, who would?

Taffy turned and looked Gabe over. "You don't have the
look of a miner," he said. His voice was not unfriendly.

"I'm not," Gabe replied.

"Well, I don't know what you're doin' here. But there's
work to be done, and if we don't get to it, we don't get paid."

Taffy showed Gabe his duties, which were simple. The tunnel floor was littered with broken rock. "You muck out," Taffy told him. "Fill the ore cars with the rock that came down in the last blast. Here's a shovel. The big pieces you pick up by hand."

So a night of backbreaking labor began for Gabe. He loaded car after car. Human mules showed up from time to time, pushing empty cars, taking away the ones Gabe had already filled, pushing them back down the tunnel, or drift, as the men called it. A portable metal plate on rollers sat near the end of the drift. It was used to turn the ore cars around. Then Gabe would start filling them up again with the blasted-out rock.

Meanwhile, Taffy and three men were drilling holes in the hard rock at the end of the drift. They used long metal rods as drills. Resting his aching back for a while, Gabe watched them work. They operated in two-man teams, one drill per team. One man held the drill point against the rock face, while his partner hit the back end with a heavy sledgehammer.

Taffy saw him watching. He let his hammer fall; perhaps he was ready for a rest, too. "We call this double-jacking," he explained. "If it's one man pounding his own drill, then it's single-jacking. We're drilling holes for the giant powder."

"That's dynamite, right?"

"Yes," Taffy replied. "Takes us an hour to go in thirty inches or so."

Taffy bent down, picked up a shorter drill about a foot long with a broad chisel point. "This is what we start the hole with. It's called a bull steel. Then, as the hole gets deeper, we use longer and thinner drills, until we get deep enough."

"Taffy," his partner prompted, "we're falling behind. Heerden will—"

"Ah, the hell with Heerden!" Taffy snapped, scowling. "A man has to act like a man, at least once in a while. And what a man does is talk. That's what makes him different from the animals, ain't it?"

The other man smiled. "Well . . . I guess that's true. At least it is with you Cousin Jacks."

Taffy spoke with a light, pleasant accent. When he saw that the term "Cousin Jack" had confused Gabe, he explained that he was a Cornishman, like a lot of the other miners. "I came all the way over here, just to go down in a hole again. . . ." Taffy shook his head ruefully.

Within a few minutes Taffy was back hammering the end of the drill. Every now and then, as the hole got deeper, either Taffy or his partner would reach into it with a long thin spoon, to scoop out the dust formed by their drilling.

From time to time, Gabe looked up to check on the progress of the drilling. There was a pattern to the holes, a pyramid shape, with extra holes out to the sides. Seven holes in all.

There was more time for talking than Gabe had expected. It was because of the heat. And the dampness. It was difficult to work for more than half an hour without resting. There were men working in the mine, usually older men, whose only job was to bring water to those working at the rock faces. And ice. Soon, Gabe found himself sucking ice with the drillers. And while they rested, Taffy, who did indeed like to talk, told him more about the mine and about mining in general. "A bad hole, this one," Taffy explained. "Hard rock mixed in with soft stuff. Which can mean cave-ins. You must have seen the sets in the big cavern."

"Sets?"

"Those big boxes of timber. Deidesheimer Square Sets. They were named after the man who designed them, a German mining engineer. If you've got a space so big you can't shore it up the normal way, you just fill it up, floor to ceiling, wall to wall, with stacks of those boxes."

Taffy told Gabe that he'd been a miner all his life. He told him about his father and one brother being killed in a cave-in, and how he'd left the Old Country to come to the new. "I had me this dream," he said rather wistfully, "of buyin' this little dab o' land, an' buildin' me a little house, with little flowers around it, marryin' me a little woman to put in the house, to help me fill it up with little children."

Taffy sighed. "But a man's gotta eat before he can build, an' the only way I know to make money for the eatin' is to be a miner. An' damned if it ain't the same here as in the Old Country. The rich own the mines and squeeze the lifeblood out of the miners."

The night dragged on and on. Like the others, Gabe was now working with his shirt off. His skin was dirty gray, where stone dust had clung to the sweat that poured out of him. The heat!

Heerden came by once. "Ah, a bunch of old women," he snarled. "My kaffirs could have done twice the work in half the time. Or I'd have had the hide off 'em."

As he walked away, one of the men muttered, "Someday, somebody's gonna kill that man."

"Why hasn't somebody?" Gabe asked.

The man looked at Gabe as if he were out of his mind. " 'Cause he'd hang, that's why. You can kill a man in a bar in a fair fight, but you lay a hand on one of the bosses, and those rich bastards will make damned sure you hang."

Finally, the shift was nearly over. Gabe had filled his last ore car, and the holes had been pounded deep enough into the rock face. A man had reached them with the day's ration of dynamite. Gabe watched as Taffy carefully worked the greasy cylinders into each hole. The dynamite trailed long fuses. "We'll blow out about a yard o' rock," Taffy explained. "All across the face. For the next shift to muck up. Then you'll muck up their work tomorrow. All for gold. Look. You can see a little seam of gold right here. Although most of it is hidden all through the rock, in flakes."

Gabe held his breath as Taffy twisted the fuses together. "Most of the time, we dig underneath the vein and let the ore fall when we set off the charge. But in this drift, we drill right into it."

He pointed upward. "There's not much rock above. Just a few yards, and then some of that soft stuff. I don't know why it hasn't come down yet to bury us. We've complained about the danger, but they say we have to go ahead and do it this way. Or get fired. That's always their big weapon. Work here, or you don't work at all. Because if you cause any trouble, then they put you on their damned blacklist, and you won't be able to find work anywhere."

Finally, the charges were set. Taffy checked his watch. "Time to light it off," he said. "We're all supposed to light our fuses at a certain time. A stupid way to do it; the whole mine should be cleared before there's any blasting. What if someone's watch is fast? Or slow? Or the blasting causes a general cave-in. But the bastards claim they'd lose too much time between shifts if we did it the safe way. So we just do it."

Taffy struck a match. The fuses, twisted together into a long rattail, took light, with a great deal of sputtering, sparks flying. "Let's get the hell out, boys!" Taffy shouted.

They moved down the drift quickly. As they passed through the big cavern, with its huge stacked timber boxes, Taffy looked up at the crumbly ceiling. "I hate soft stuff," he murmured.

Quite a number of men had gathered near the lift cage. Taffy checked his watch again. "Any moment now," he said.

Then Gabe heard it, felt it, a distant rumble, pushing at his eardrums, his whole body. The floor shook. There were more rumblings as other charges fired in a ragged salvo. Dust poured out of tunnel mouths. "We should be above ground," Taffy muttered.

Heerden, who was standing nearby, overhead. "What's the matter, little man?" he sneered. "Are you afraid?"

Taffy looked at him with open contempt. "Any miner who isn't afraid is gonna be a dead miner."

"Ya?" Heerden said, his face flushing with anger. "Maybe you should be afraid of me."

He took a step toward Taffy. Taffy did not back away. The other men closed in slightly. Some were carrying hammers. The air filled with tension. Heerden looked puzzled; usually, the men backed down. Then he remembered all this talk about forming a union. "Ah," he muttered. "If you were my kaffirs . . ."

Then he turned and walked into the cage. The men followed. The cage lurched upward, driving Gabe's stomach down toward his feet. Thank God, he thought. In another couple of minutes, I'll be breathing fresh air again.

The cage jerked to a halt. But it was still dark outside. Gabe saw that they had stopped at the opening of one of the upper drifts.

"You," Heerden said, motioning to Gabe. "Come with me."

Puzzled, Gabe followed Heerden out of the cage. Somebody tugged on a signal rope, and the cage shot up again.

Heerden and Gabe were alone in the drift. It was an old drift; even Gabe could see that it had not been worked in some time. Heerden led Gabe into the drift for a few yards. They stopped at a small side chamber, perhaps a false start toward a vein that had eventually played out. A mattress had been placed on the floor, along with a big jug of water and a pot of stew. "This is where you live from now on," Heerden said. "I pick you up tomorrow, when it's time for your shift."

Gabe stared at Heerden. There was a cold, malicious glint in Heerden's little eyes. "It could be worse," Heerden said. "It's a little cooler up here."

Gabe wanted to push past Heerden, head for the main shaft. But what good would it do him? The cage had already left. Heerden seemed to read his mind. "There are guards up above," he said. "Like you used to be. They have orders to shoot you on sight if you show your face above ground."

Gabe had been considering killing Heerden, then grabbing the next lift cage. But he didn't know how to call it. He felt sick, panicky, at the thought of being buried down here day and night. But he forced himself to calm down. As he had been taught in his youth, his face showed nothing. Never, never let the enemy see that you feel pain.

"I'll see you tomorrow," he said quietly.

Heerden showed surprise at Gabe's mild tone. And a little disappointment. Perhaps, Gabe thought, he wanted to hear me beg. It's you who will beg someday, Heerden, he silently promised, in the last moments of your miserable life.

A few minutes later he was alone. He sat down and began to eat his stew while he could still see to do so. He'd already looked at the level of oil in his lamp, and knew that it would soon go out. Another refinement in his punishment. Darkness.

His thoughts turned to Jennings. After Heerden, you'll be next, Jennings, he vowed. But I may not give you time to beg.

CHAPTER ELEVEN

No longer able to tell day from night, Gabe quickly became disoriented in time. There was only sleep and work. Heerden left him in the abandoned drift the whole twelve hours, every time he was off shift, most of that time in the dark. The work itself, the company of the miners, even the dim light of the lanterns, became the focus of his life, all he had to look forward to.

The other men noticed, of course, Gabe's prisoner status. Many had already recognized him as one of the guards. At first, some thought he might have been sent down the hole to spy on them. Then the word trickled along, from Peterson, that he was a man to be trusted.

But that did not make Gabe's life any easier. He knew he would eventually have to make a break for freedom, or he would slowly lose his mind, trapped in this hot, hellish hole.

He and Taffy became very close. Taffy constantly filled Gabe in on what was happening on the surface, or topside as he called it. "The men are gettin' fed up," Taffy said one night, while the crew was resting, gulping water and sucking ice. "There's word that they're gonna cut down the hired help and up our quotas. They haven't cut our wages yet, but there's talk they definitely will."

"How the hell could they get the men to work harder than they're already working?" Gabe wondered aloud.

"Fear," Taffy replied. "Fear of losing your job. And fear of dyin'. One of the guards killed a miner two days ago. Claimed the miner came at him with a hammer in his hand. That almost touched off a riot. But that damned Jennings was there, with his men, all armed with shotguns. And from the look on Jennings's face, they were ready for a massacre."

Taffy shook his head. "That one blew over, but there's only so much the men can take. If they don't let up the pressure, there *will* be a massacre. But who's gonna be doin' the massacring, I don't know."

The conversation was cut off by Heerden's arrival. He snarled at the men to get back to work. They responded, but in a sullen manner, which further enraged Heerden, who stalked away, swearing viciously.

Day after day, more backbreaking work. There were occasional diversions. Once, when Gabe and Taffy had left the cage at the beginning of their shift and were walking through the huge cavern stacked with its giant boxes, Gabe was startled by an enormous uproar coming from one side, a wild, screaming hammering, one of the most inhuman sounds he had ever heard. "What—" he started to say.

Taffy grimaced. "Ah, it's the damned widow-makers. They're startin' to bring 'em into this mine. That's why so many of the men are worried about their jobs—with the widow-makers, they'll need fewer men for the drillin'."

"Widow-makers?"

"Come on," Taffy said. "I'll show you."

He waved the other men in his crew toward the drift they were working, then led Gabe off to the right. The sound was coming from a drift on the far side of the big cavern. It was a shallow drift, but large across. Huge clouds of dust were pouring out of the entrance.

Taffy led the way inside. A small steam engine was chuffing away just inside the entrance. Hoses snaked away from the engine. It was hard to see, with all the dust, but when Taffy had led Gabe a little further into the drift, he saw two men standing in front of the blank stone at the end of the workings, holding, between them, a large contraption that was connected to the hoses. The hammering noise was coming from the contraption, which to Gabe looked a little like a huge gun.

"A compressed-air drill," Taffy said, during a lull in the hammering, while the men moved the drill bit to another location. "Does the work of several men. And does it fast. If you can stand up to the hammering."

The drill started up again. Gabe watched the two men who were running it. They were big men, with sweat running down their mostly naked bodies, muscles straining as they leaned into the drill, pressing it forward. Gabe watched as the drill chewed its way into the rock. There was something heroic about the men's concentration in their handling of the machine.

Taffy was tugging at Gabe's arm. They left the drift. When they reached the big cavern, Gabe's ears were still ringing from the sound of the air drill. He thought of the men, the way they were tearing holes into the mountain. Apparently, there were no limits to what the White Man could do, once he wanted to rip something up. Then, as they walked toward their own drift, he remembered what Taffy had called the drill. "Why do they call it a widow-maker?" he asked.

Taffy grimaced. "Because of the dust. Little chips of rock dust. With so much of it flying around, it gets into the lungs. Causes a disease called silicosis. Little by little your lungs fill up, and you stop breathing, until eventually you slowly suffocate to death. Hard on the miners, but oh, it makes a pile of money for those filthy rich bastards."

Taffy looked over at Gabe. He'd never pried into Gabe's business, but he now said, "With what Jennings and the rest seem to have against ya, lad, it's a wonder they don't put ya on a widow-maker. Or worse. Maybe in the stamp mill topside, where the mercury they use will do even worse things to a man than an air drill."

Gabe nodded, although he could not understand how anything could be worse than being cut off from air and light. From the sky, the wind, from life itself.

Later that day, while he was working hard, shoveling rock and gravel into an ore car, he became aware that the others had stopped their drilling. They were all looking back down the drift. Gabe looked up. A group of men walked out of the darkness, only two of them carrying lanterns. The rest were loaded down with weapons.

Jennings was a step out ahead of the newcomers. He stopped about eight feet away from Gabe, thumbs hooked in his gun belt, a sneer on his face as he took in Gabe's dirt-smeared, sweaty body. "You look more natural doin' this, Conrad," he said, chuckling.

Gabe said nothing, just stood, looking straight back at Jennings. His steady stare made Jennings a little nervous; he could see, in those otherwise expressionless eyes, the cold desire to kill. "Tell you what, Conrad," Jennings said. "If you come clean about you and Peterson, what happened to Ace and Buck, I'll take you out of this stinking hole."

"No thanks," Gabe said drily. "I'd rather be here, three thousand feet down, than six feet under, topside."

Jennings held his hands out to the side in mock surprise. "Conrad," he said, "how come I get the impression you don't trust me?"

Gabe did not reply; there was really nothing to say.

Then Jennings stopped his clowning. "You son of a bitch," he said to Gabe. "My problem is that I *did* trust you. And I keep gettin' the feelin' you suckered me. Nobody suckers me, Conrad, and gets away with it."

Still, Gabe said nothing. Realizing that he wasn't going to get the satisfaction of watching Gabe beg, Jennings snorted, turned on his heel, and stalked away down the drift. The four gunmen with him remained in place for a few seconds, shotguns in hand, alert for any trouble. Only when they were certain that the miners were not going to react did they finally turn and start away. Except for one man, who continued to watch Gabe.

"Conrad," the man finally said. "You always were a holier-than-thou pain in the ass. It looks good, seeing you taken down a few notches." The man laughed loudly. "A hell of a *lotta* notches."

Then he turned and briskly walked away, catching up to the others. Gabe, watching him go, was aware of Taffy, standing next to him. "If we could only tell when they're comin' down," Taffy murmured. "We could make life interestin' for 'em. Maybe arrange a special little cave-in."

"You watch yourself, Taffy," Gabe warned. "They play for keeps."

"So do I," Taffy replied, then turned back to his work, banging his hammer extra-hard against the drill.

At the end of the shift, when Heerden met Gabe at the lift cage, he was even more arrogant than usual. "I got the word, Conrad. You're gonna stay down here until there ain't nothin' left to take back topside."

Gabe looked away. He knew that Heerden was trying to bait him. The big South African had been pushing him for some time, hoping he could goad Gabe into swinging on him. Gabe was tempted, but realized that even if he won the fight, he'd lose overall. Maybe get put onto a widow-maker crew. Or left in his isolated upper drift, alone, for days. However, looking into Heerden's piggish little eyes, he began to consider that it might be worth it. The pleasure of smashing in that ugly face . . .

The men were all standing around, exhausted, impatient. The lift cage had already taken one load of men up. It was probably at the top by now. Gabe was watching Heerden intently, waiting for the foreman to say one thing, just one more thing, when his attention was diverted by a sudden tension among the miners. "Ah, no," he heard Taffy say. "For the love o' God, not again."

Then Gabe heard it, too, from far above, a drawn-out, terrified scream, very faint at first, but growing louder as it drew nearer. He did not understand for a moment, then realized. Someone was falling down the shaft!

The scream cut off into a grunt as the man's body struck something, perhaps an outcrop of rock or the edge of a tunnel entrance. Now the man started to ricochet off other obstructions. There were more heavy thuds, growing closer. Then, to the horror of the waiting men, a terrible rain started. A rain of blood and body parts. An arm. A chunk of torso. The men scattered, getting out of the way.

There was a void below the point where the lift cage made its stop, a deep sump, designed the catch the huge volume of water that constantly seeped into the diggings. Most of the man's body fell into this sump. Gabe could hear individual splashes, far below.

When nothing more came down the shaft, the men clustered around, looking down. Steam rose out of the sump. "The water's really hot down there," Taffy said to Gabe, his voice hushed. "Not far from boiling. Kind of cooks a body, real slow. The meat comes right off the bone. They'll have to fish the poor bastard out with hooks, chunk by chunk. If they bother."

Taffy looked up the shaft, into the blackness. "After all the heat down here, and the pressure, you can get dizzy when you get to the top. That's when you're most likely to fall. Of course, the bastards won't spend a penny for any safety equipment. Or let the men work shorter shifts. It would cut into their goddamned profits."

"That's enough, Taffy," Heerden said. But Gabe could tell from his voice that he was shaken up, too, although he tried not to show it.

They were all quiet then. The only sound as they waited for their turn in the lift cage was the hissing steam rising from the sump.

CHAPTER TWELVE

Even though he was buried deep in the mine, Gabe was aware of developments topside. The miners, previously closemouthed about their troubles, were now talking openly about the union, about wages, about their troubles with the company men, like Heerden and Jennings.

It quickly became clear that Taffy was fully committed to the idea of a union. "When I left the Old Country," he said one day, while the crew was resting, "they were hangin' men for union talk. I thought there might be a better chance here, in the land o' liberty."

He snorted. "But ye get the same bunch o' rich bastards, payin' off the politicians, squeezin' the workin'man."

The mood of the men became worse as the mine owners, suffering from bad business decisions in other ventures, tried to force a greater profit out of the mine. Instead of planning for greater efficiency, they simply decided to work the miners harder. For less money. And with an even greater disregard for safety.

To save time during the shift changeover, the word came down from the top that the period of waiting between blasting and reentering the drifts would be shortened. The owners would gain an extra working hour a day out of the men.

Taffy could not, at first, believe it. "They're playin' with our lives," he muttered. "For a few dollars gain."

"Is it that dangerous?" Gabe asked.

Taffy spat. "There's a reason for that waitin'. Sometimes there's a hang-fire. A fuse doesn't burn right, maybe smolders for a while, then starts up again. Goes off minutes or even half an hour late. Pity the poor miner who goes back early. Or another kind of thing can happen that's just as bad, maybe worse. The blast cracks the rock, all right, but it just hangs there for a while, till the strain gets too great, and it finally falls. That's the main reason we wait. To let the drift settle out after the blast. And to let the dust clear. It's bad for the lungs, the dust, and it can flare up, explode, if there's enough of it in the air. Just a spark, and . . . boom!"

A formal complaint was lodged with the foremen. Not as formal a complaint as it would have been if they'd already had a recognized union, but still, a complaint. The men waited sullenly while an older miner delivered the complaint at the pithead. No one actually said they were refusing to go down the shaft, but no one moved toward the cage, either.

The foremen—there were six of them—milled around together, out of earshot of the men, talking vehemently. From time to time Heerden's voice could be heard, apparently demanding that all the men at the pithead be fired on the spot.

But then, of course, there would be no one to work that shift. And with no ore brought up, there would be no profits for their masters back East. Finally, the foremen promised they would relay the complaint to the mine superintendent. After the men went to work.

So down the shaft they went. Once at the rock face, Taffy told Gabe about the confrontation. "So they said they'd take it to the superintendent," he snorted. "He's a useless drunk. Got no guts of his own."

It was three days before the word came back, telegraphed from the East. The men would do as they were told. Any who refused would be fired on the spot. The message was really a threat, promising that the company would shut the mine down if it had to and bring in scabs from the East. No damned miners were going to interfere with the owners' God-given property rights.

A few men quit. But the rest went down the hole. Gabe heard that Peterson, constantly on the move to keep out of the way of Jennings's thugs, was pressing even harder for a union. That was perhaps the only reason the men went back down—the possibility that something would be done soon.

For two days all went well. Gabe's shift headed straight for their drifts while the shocks from the previous shift's blasting were still reverberating throughout the mine. Little time was gained; the dust was so thick for the first half hour that the men could hardly see to work. Or breathe.

On the second day, Gabe could see that Taffy was worried. He kept glancing up at the rock ceiling above them. "I don't like it," he said. "I think the rock's getting thinner up there, that it's sloping downward the deeper we go into the drift. I don't think there's much above us, holding back that soft stuff."

Taffy complained to Heerden. The South African sneered. "You Cousin Jacks," he said. "No guts. Maybe you see things under your bed, too."

So nothing was done. On the third day, as the sound of the blasts died away, the crew started toward their diggings. "You!" Heerden said, stopping Gabe. "I got news for you."

The others had stopped, too. Heerden scowled, then snarled, "The rest of you get to work! You don't get paid for standin' around."

Taffy and the others started toward the drift. Gabe turned toward Heerden. The big South African was grinning. "They figure you got it too easy as a mucker," he said, obviously enjoying himself. "You go on the air drill tomorrow. Then we see how tough you are."

Gabe said nothing, just turned and walked away. He realized that he was going to have to get out of the mine, make his break, even if it cost him his life. With Heerden breathing down his neck, he'd be finished soon enough, anyway.

He was just entering the drift when he heard a loud rumble ahead, followed by the crash of falling stone. Then, he heard men screaming.

A blast of new dust rushed toward him. He dropped to the floor of the drift, coughing, but found breathable air. Then, as soon as he was certain he could breathe, he rushed down the drift.

A chest-high wall of rock lay across his path. He looked up. As Taffy had feared, part of the ceiling had fallen in, not pulverized rock, as from the blasting, but big slabs, some weighing tons. Still, there was room to crawl over the rock. Clawing his way, Gabe scrambled toward the back of the drift. From behind him he could hear shouting and the sound of running feet. Others had heard the rockfall and were on their way to help.

The end of the drift was still clear; only part of the ceiling had come down. Gabe saw an arm protruding out of a pile of rock. Nothing more was visible of whoever was under all that rock, other than a huge pool of blood, seeping out onto the floor.

A groan came from up ahead. Gabe crawled over some more rock, expecting to find the rest of the crew huddled against the end of the tunnel. No one. No one in sight except Taffy. And when Gabe saw his friend, he immediately wished he hadn't.

Taffy was pinned beneath a huge slab of rock, from the middle of his torso on down. From the way the slab lay, from its closeness to the tunnel floor, Taffy's lower body was obviously crushed flat.

Yet he was still alive. Gabe crawled over to Taffy, saw that his friend recognized him. "Gabe," Taffy started to say, reaching out with a filthy, bloodstained hand, but the effort moved something inside Taffy's crushed body, and he suddenly let out a terrible cry, while blood bubbled from his mouth.

Men crowded in. One man retched when he saw what was left of Taffy. Others immediately started hunting for the rest of the crew, but, other than that single arm, they were buried out of sight beneath the rubble. Still, the men began digging, trying to prize stones away with digging bars, grunting over their task, their eyes wild.

A couple of men came up with other bars, ready to pry the huge block off Taffy's lower body. Taffy had quieted down, but when they did manage to move the stone a little, he let out another wild cry of agony.

The men stepped back. Gabe saw that one of them was crying. Gabe knelt down by Taffy's head. "If we don't move it . . ." he said.

Taffy was breathing in great, ragged gasps. "And if you do," he murmured, "it'll end the same."

Gabe heard his friend grinding his teeth together. "Ah, God, Gabe," Taffy whispered. "For God's sake, end it for me. Hit me over the head. Do something. The pain. The bloody pain. . . ."

Suddenly, Gabe felt a rough hand on his shoulder. He looked up. Heerden was standing above him. "The stupid bastard," Heerden snarled. "What did he go and do?"

Gabe stood up slowly, turned so that he was facing Heerden squarely. "It's not what he did, but what you didn't do," he said, his voice grating with tension. "When he told you about the stone above our drift, you laughed. Are you laughing now, Heerden?"

Heerden started to look away, then forced himself to meet Gabe's gaze. Perhaps if he had apologized, or even looked horror-struck, the tension might have lessened. But Heerden's personality, forged in the brutal conditions of South Africa, where ugly acts were routinely performed with the justification that that was the way God had ordained it, could not permit himself to feel remorse. "You shut your stinking mouth, Conrad. I'll bury you so deep in this mine, that—"

Gabe hit him flush in the face. So hard that his hand hurt. Yet Heerden might not have gone down if his heel had not caught on a chunk of rock. Blood spurted from a cut on his cheek, but as he hit the floor, he was already rolling, and when he leapt to his feet, he tore one of the five foot long digging bars from a man's hands. "By God, Conrad," he snarled, wiping blood from his face with the back of his hand, "for that, I kill you."

He lunged toward Gabe, swinging the digging bar. Gabe stepped back. The bar clanged off rock, striking sparks. Heerden charged again, swinging the bar downward at Gabe's head. Gabe dodged to one side, managing to slip past Heerden.

"Here," one of the miners said. Gabe felt cold steel against the flesh of his right hand. One of the miners had handed him a rock drill. Four feet of steel. Heerden was already turning, readying the digging bar. Gabe lunged forward, swinging the drill, smashing it against Heerden's shoulder. Heerden cried out, staggered, dropped the digging bar, one shoulder sagging low, broken bones jutting through torn flesh.

Gabe struck again, smashing Heerden's left knee. Howling with pain, Heerden fell onto his side, thrashing in agony, but he managed to turn over onto his back. His eyes widened in fear as he saw Gabe, standing above him, with the drill held high. Heerden tried to raise his hands to protect his head, but only one arm would work.

Gabe changed his grip on the drill, so that he was holding it by the butt, with the chisel-shaped tip pointed straight downward. He thrust with all his strength. Taffy had always been meticulous about keeping his drills sharp. The point entered Heerden's body at the navel. Gabe struck so hard that the drill passed all the way through Heerden's body. The tip clanged loudly against the rock floor.

Heerden grunted, his eyes bulging. He looked down to where the drill protruded from his body. Gabe let go of the drill. Its weight made it sag to one side, and as it tore at the deep wound in Heerden's guts, Heerden screamed, a high, shrill note of agony.

Turning from Heerden, Gabe knelt by Taffy again. To his surprise, Taffy was smiling. "I'm glad I lasted long enough to see that," Taffy whispered. Then he died. The light simply faded out of his eyes, and he was no longer breathing.

Gabe stood up. When he turned around, Heerden was grunting and thrashing, trying, with his one good arm, to pull the drill from his body. A man stepped forward, as if to help. "Don't," Gabe snapped. Startled, the man looked up into Gabe's eyes. He recoiled from their intensity and stepped back.

Another man took Gabe by the arm. "You'll have to get out of here," the man said. He gestured toward Heerden. "They'll have your head for this."

Gabe nodded and began to climb back over the pile of stone. He found a mob of men milling about on the far side. "Is there anyone still alive in there?" one man asked.

Gabe shook his head. "All dead. Four of them."

A horrible scream came from the far side of the rock slide. A bubbling, wailing scream of agony, as the drill bit tore at Heerden's intestines. One of the miners, shocked, asked Gabe, "But I thought you said they were all—"

"Four are. That one will take a long time dying."

The scream seemed to trigger something inside the miners. "Those bastards!" someone shouted. "Forcing good men to risk their lives!"

More shouting arose. Men began to mill about. "We gotta shut this mine down, boys!" someone called out. "Keep 'em from killin' off the rest of us!"

"Let's get topside," someone else called out. "Before Jennings's henchmen get organized."

There was a rush toward the lift cage. Gabe let the crowd carry him along. By the time the cage started up, it was packed to capacity. Gabe was sandwiched in the middle, barely able to draw breath. But breathe he did when the cage finally reached the top. Fresh air. Fresh, cool air, the first he'd breathed in a long time.

The men rushed out of the cage. Two of Jennings's guards were on duty. One raised his rifle, but the men were all over him and his companion. The guard got off one shot, toward the ceiling, then the rifle was ripped from his hands. The last

Gabe saw of the guards, they had gone down beneath a pile of punching, kicking miners.

Time to go. He had to keep moving, and moving fast. Jennings would bring reinforcements. Gabe doubted that even all of Jennings's guards would be able to contain the rage of the miners, but if they recognized him, he'd probably be shot down on sight.

But first they'd have to see him, and Gabe had spent his whole life training to move unseen.

It was still more than an hour short of dawn. Gabe had little trouble slipping through the dark streets, just one man among the dozens of excited miners running through the town. He picked up a coil of rope hanging from a peg at the blacksmith's shop, then he slipped through back alleys until he reached the high palisade at the back of Jennings's fort. He made a loop in the rope and threw it upward. He tried twice before it snagged on one of the logs. A few seconds later he had climbed up to the top of the palisade.

A quick look revealed pandemonium inside the fort, men rushing into the armory, seizing weapons. Gabe watched Jennings marshal his gunmen, then lead them out the main gate.

The fort was practically deserted. Gabe dropped down onto the roof of the stables, landing softly on his moccasins. He held very still for several seconds, but no one had noticed him.

It was easy to slip into the stables unseen. His big, black stallion was still in its stall. The horse snuffled loudly when it spotted Gabe. He quickly saddled and bridled the animal, then strapped the saddle scabbards into place. Satisfied, he left the horse in its stall and slipped back out into the night.

Good. In all the excitement they hadn't thought to lock the armory door. Gabe slipped inside. To his relief, all his weapons were there; his two rifles in the rifle racks, with his gun belt and holsters draped over the muzzles, complete with pistols. The rifles were unloaded. He strapped on the pistols, then quickly loaded them with ammunition from the gun belt's cartridge loops. Picking up his rifles, he hurried to the armory door.

Not much moving outside. The few guards left behind were focusing most of their attention on the main gate. Gabe slipped outside, walked quickly across the tiny yard, toward the barracks door. Pushing the door open, he walked straight inside.

There were two men in the barracks. One, spotting Gabe, started to shout and reach for his pistol. Gabe clouted the man across the side of the head with the barrel of his Winchester. The man went down, groaning, his pistol clattering onto the floor. Gabe quickly covered the other man, who had, so far, made no move.

"Hey!" the man said quickly. "I got no fight with you, Conrad. I'm on my way outta here. This whole operation's comin' apart at the seams."

Then Gabe saw that the man had been shoving his belongings into saddlebags. "Take out your pistol," Gabe said. "Real slow, and drop it on the floor."

The man shrugged, pulled out his pistol using only the tips of his fingers, then bent down to lay it carefully on the floor. Meanwhile, Gabe had moved over to the man he'd hit and kicked his pistol under a bed. The man was sitting up now, holding his head in both hands. Blood was trickling down the side of his face. "If you give me any trouble at all," Gabe said quietly, "either of you, I'll kill you instantly."

The man who'd dropped his gun shrugged, then sat down on a bunk. Gabe left the other man sitting in the middle of the floor and moved over to his bunk, but saw nothing in sight. "Where's my gear?" he asked the man on the bunk.

The man motioned to the far corner of the room. "In the locker."

There were large cupboards at the end of the room. Gabe opened two doors before he found his saddlebags and bedroll. Rummaging through them, he discovered that everything seemed to be there. He heard a low chuckle from the man on the bunk. "Jennings said he'd shoot any man who stole your stuff. We believed him. He's a strange breed o' cat, Jennings."

Yes, he definitely was. Gabe picked up his slouch hat and settled it onto his head. The duster was there, too. He put it on over the shoulder rig, then he took shells out of the saddlebags and loaded both rifles. Slinging his saddlebags and bedroll over his shoulder, he started toward the door, a rifle in each hand. Near the door, he hesitated, then turned to face the two men. The man on the bunk was watching him nervously. The man sitting on the floor now had a dirty bandanna pressed against the cut on the side of his head, where Gabe's rifle barrel had landed. He looked like he'd had all the fight knocked out of him. "Both of you," Gabe said. "I could kill you now, or maybe tie you up. But I'm going to leave you where you are. However, if either of you shows his face outside this door within the next five minutes, I'll kill you for sure."

The man on the bunk nodded. "Yeah, Conrad. I believe you. You're a strange breed o' cat, too."

Gabe slipped outside and returned to the stable. His horse was stamping nervously inside the stall. It took Gabe only a couple of minutes to strap the remainder of his gear into place. Then he mounted and rode the animal right up to the stable's exit. Now would come the hard part. Fighting his way out of the fort. Common sense should have dictated that he not even come here, but there were things in his saddlebags and bedroll that he valued. Like Two Face's pipe.

He was considering simply riding up to the gate, drawing down on the gate guards, and demanding they open up. He should be able to take them by surprise; after all, they were primarily worried about danger from outside, not from behind. Still, there might be a fight, and then he would be trapped inside the fort with people shooting at him from all sides.

Events solved his problem. Suddenly Gabe heard a lot of yelling from outside. "Open the goddamn gate!" a voice shouted. "We gotta get under cover!"

Then Gabe heard another voice shouting, Jennings's voice. "Come on back here, you yella-livered sons o' bitches!"

So, some of the gunmen were running scared. Not Jennings, obviously. Confused, the guards swung the gate partway open, giving Gabe his opportunity. The gates were still moving when he jammed his heels into his horse's flanks. The big black, already excited from all the noise and Gabe's obvious tension, shot forward.

Gabe was halfway to the gate before the guards even became aware of him. Since he was coming from inside the fort, they paid no attention at first. Gabe was almost level with the gate before they realized who it was. "Goddamn!" one guard shouted. "It's Conrad!"

Gabe pulled out his Winchester. He did not fire, but simply used the barrel to club men aside. His horse knocked into two men, sending them flying. Then Gabe was outside, racing through a group of several gunmen who were so intent on reaching the safety of the fort they hardly noticed him.

Gabe was vaguely aware of a mob of men a hundred yards away. Miners. And they were armed. Bright spots of flame were visible as the miners fired at the gunmen. Jennings was between the miners and his own men, trying to rally a defense, but his men were out of control. Particularly now, with Gabe riding among them, clubbing men down. "Conrad!" Jennings shouted. "You son of a bitch!"

He raised his rifle. Gabe tried to bring up the Winchester, but Jennings fired first. Gabe felt a hammer blow against his left side, low on the ribs. He swayed in the saddle, almost dropped his rifle, but managed to steady himself. He heard another bullet whiz by his head, then, veering to the right, he rode into an alleyway, where he was protected by the corner of a building. Just in time. Jennings had rallied his men. A volley of shots splintered wood from the building's walls.

Gabe rode down the alley at a slow trot. His side felt numb. Reaching down, he felt slippery warmth. He checked his breathing. Smooth enough; at least they hadn't gotten him through the lungs, No, not they. Jennings. It had been Jennings's bullet that had hit him.

He was tempted to ride on out of town, find a quiet spot, check his wound. It was beginning to grow light; he'd have no trouble finding his way.

Instead, he rode toward the town's center. Gabe had no intention of leaving. He had a score to settle.

CHAPTER THIRTEEN

He found Peterson at the town's single rattletrap hotel. Gabe had no trouble making it through the streets; despite the fact that he was once again fully armed and outfitted, he had by now become identified to the miners as one of their own.

Peterson was in the hotel's small lobby, surrounded by miners, calmly issuing orders. He was surprised when he saw Gabe. "I figured you'd be long gone."

"Nope," Gabe replied. "I don't figure it's over quite yet."

"How right you are," Peterson said ruefully. "When the . . ."

Then he noticed the big patch of blood on the side of Gabe's duster. "Are you hurt?" he asked, obviously concerned.

"I got hit coming out of the fort," Gabe replied laconically. He was already shrugging out of his duster. Damn, it hurt to move.

Peterson helped him take off his shirt, which was wet with blood. Now Gabe could see the wound, a long, shallow gash in his side where Jennings's bullet had bounced off a rib. Good. Not a very serious wound. As long as it didn't become infected. He looked up at Peterson, who had a strained look on his face. Understandable. Peterson was a planner, an organizer. The realities of wounds, of blood, and eventually, of dead men, were fairly new to him. "I'll send for the town doctor," Peterson said.

"No time," Gabe replied. "If you could get some water . . ."

A basin was brought. Gabe leaned back, sponged the wound as clean as he could. It was even shallower than he'd thought. "Is there any alcohol around?" he asked.

"Whiskey?" an old miner asked, grinning, imagining Gabe wanted it for the pain.

"Uh-uh. Ethyl alcohol would be better."

Taking control again, Peterson sent a man over to the store for the alcohol. "And bring a new shirt," he added, tossing Gabe's torn, bloody shirt into a corner.

The man was back within five minutes. A dozen men watched as Gabe poured alcohol into his wound. They were all aware, as the alcohol washed over Gabe's side, that his expression did not change at all. It hurt, though. Hurt like hell. But Gabe kept the pain private.

The man who'd gone to the store also brought a length of cotton cloth. Peterson helped wrap it around Gabe's ribs. It felt good to have the wound covered. While he was putting on the new shirt, he turned toward Peterson. "What are you doing about Jennings?" he asked.

Peterson hesitated. "Why . . . we already ran him out of town. . . ."

"But what about the fort? Do you know what he's doing? Are you keeping an eye on him?"

"I . . . don't know. Do you think he'll—"

"Attack us, yes," Gabe finished for Peterson. "And probably within the next half hour. Come on, let's go take a look."

As Gabe had expected, the miners, inexperienced in fighting, had made the usual mistake of thinking of their enemy as already defeated. No one was really watching the fort; some of the men had already broken into a bar and were starting to drink. "We've got to get the men back into position," Gabe insisted.

He watched while Peterson cajoled about twenty men to pick up their guns again and fan out, facing the fort's main gate. Gabe walked quickly back to his horse. In a few minutes he was back, carrying his Sharps and a sack of cartridges. "Anything happening?" he asked Peterson.

Peterson pointed toward a tall tower where canvas hoses were hung to dry. "Got a man up there. He can see right down into the fort."

Cupping his hands around his mouth, Peterson called up, "Hey, Hal! See anything?"

A face appeared at a small opening high in the tower. "Lotsa people movin' around," the man called down. "Horses and all."

"They're going to try to rush out, mounted," Gabe said. "Maybe sweep around to the side and come at us from behind. Ride right through town, panic your men, and get them to break. Then they can pick off your people at will."

Peterson looked worried. "Do you think it'll work?"

"Yes. If they make it out of the fort in good order. Look," he said, "what you've got to do is make it too hot for them to show their noses. Keep them pinned inside. Or surround them just as they ride out, gun them down from cover, although it takes steady nerves to stand up to mounted men, charging straight at you. I don't know if your miners—"

"No," Peterson said emphatically. "We've got to avoid killing. If there's a big bloodbath, the army'll be on us right away. We'll be in the wrong. We have to keep from looking like butchers."

Gabe nodded. He understood Peterson's viewpoint. He wanted to build something. A union. Decent wages and conditions for his miners. He was unlikely to gain his objectives through slaughter. Gabe, however, had a different goal—Jennings's hide. "All right," he said. "Then you have to keep them pinned down, where they can't do any harm."

Gabe knew time was running out. He helped Peterson position his men until a good thirty guns were facing the fort's main gate. Jennings had made a mistake in his choice

of a site for the fort. It was too close to the town. The main
gate was within easy rifle shot of many of the buildings, with
plenty of cover for riflemen. Probably Jennings had never
anticipated that the situation would ever deteriorate this far,
that the miners would rise in revolt, face down his gunmen.

Jennings made his move within minutes after Gabe had
posted the last rifleman. Gabe heard the solid clunk of the big
bar being taken down from behind the fort's gate. A moment
later the gate began to swing open. Gabe waited until it was
open only a couple of yards, then he shouted, "Fire!"

Thirty repeating rifles roared. With the men working the
loading levers as fast as they could, a storm of lead struck
the partially open gate. Two horsemen had already started to
ride through. Their horses were killed beneath them, slammed
backward by a fusillade of bullets. The firing died away for a
few seconds as men rammed more cartridges into their rifles'
loading gates. Gabe could hear panicked shouting from inside
the fort, the scream of a wounded horse, the cursing of a man
who'd been hit. "Close the damn gate!" someone called out, as
another fusillade slammed against the gate's thick timbers.

The gate slammed shut, but the miners, excited, kept
firing. Gabe had to call out several times before the firing
died away. Peterson, standing next to Gabe just behind the
corner of a building, muttered, "Well . . . they sure as hell
didn't get out."

"Nope. Not this time. But we've gotta keep up the
pressure."

Remembering his own coming and going from the fort,
Gabe suggested to Peterson that he post a guard near the
fort's rear wall so no one could escape that way and perhaps work around behind the miners watching the front
gate.

After the firing, it now seemed very quiet. Quiet enough
for Gabe to hear a voice call out from inside the fort, "Conrad!
I know you're out there. That had to be you, setting up
that little surprise. Peterson couldn't shoot his way out of
a cardboard box."

Gabe said nothing. It was best to let Jennings keep guessing.

"Conrad!" Jennings called out again. "You can't win. We represent too damned much power. The mine owners'll send a small army. You'll be wiped out."

Peterson stepped close to the corner of the building and shouted back, "And how the hell are they going to know about it, Jennings? We took over the telegraph office. You can't get word out."

Gabe smiled. Peterson was learning. What he'd just said, so loudly, was more for the benefit of Jennings's men than for Jennings himself. If they thought they were totally cut off, maybe they'd give up. Maybe they'd mutiny, desert.

But Jennings reply was unequivocal. "Go to hell!" he shouted. "I'll see you both hang. Along with any goddamn miner that picks up a gun."

Meant for the miners this time. Gabe looked around, saw concern on some faces. But, as long as they were winning, the miners would probably hold onto their courage. On the other hand, a single setback might be enough to break them.

There was no more shouting from the fort. Gabe figured Jennings was probably back in his office, planning and plotting, dreaming of Gabe and Peterson swinging from a gallows. As long as Jennings was alive, he was dangerous.

Gabe looked over at Peterson. From the worried look on his face, he was probably coming to the same conclusion. He saw Gabe watching him. "Well?" he asked. "Now what?"

Gabe looked down at himself, saw how filthy he was. Dirt from all that time inside the mine was ground into his skin. His hair was stiff with sweat and dust. "Well, I don't know about you," he said, smiling, "but I sure as hell could use a bath."

Seeing the surprise on Peterson's face, he added. "There's plenty of time."

He turned toward the fort. "That's going to be one hell of a hard nut to crack."

*   *   *

Gabe was back with Peterson by noon. Not only had he bathed, but he had also purchased new trousers and another shirt. He still wore the same duster, with the side stained with blood; there had been no other available.

Peterson had set up a core of sharpshooters facing the fort's gates, backed up by riflemen, in case Jennings tried another sortie. The men were rotated every two hours so they did not lose their edge. There were plenty of miners eager to have their shot at the men who'd terrorized them for so long.

Peterson was in an ebullient mood; tactics seemed to energize him. "I'm having a contraption made," he informed Gabe. He pointed back down an alley where men were winding lengths of heavy rope between two squat uprights. "It's a catapult," he said proudly. "They may have a lot of guns in their fort, but we've got something they haven't. Dynamite."

Gabe watched as a thick plank was inserted between the strands of rope. A crude basket was attached to the upper end of the plank. Men heaved away on a block and tackle, and the plank was bent backward. As it moved, the ropes holding it in place began to twist. Gabe could hear them creaking from the strain.

The makeshift catapult was moved close to the corner, behind a wall that was just high enough to protect the men setting up their contraption but low enough to permit it to hurl its deadly projectiles. "They should have wound it up after they moved it," Peterson worried out loud. But it didn't go off prematurely. Gabe watched as a miner placed a bundle made up of three sticks of dynamite into the basket. He lit the fuse. "Let 'er rip!" the man shouted, running to the side.

A man released a catch. The plank jerked upright, slamming against a heavy cross beam. The dynamite soared into the air, clear over the fort, trailing sparks. A moment later there was a loud blast from the far side of the fort. Heads popped up above the walls, until Peterson's snipers spotted them and began firing.

After that, it was simply a matter of trying to figure out how much tension to place against the plank and the ropes. First, they over-corrected, and the dynamite fell short, detonating near the fort's log wall. Since the blast was not contained, most of its force was wasted straight upward.

But the men inside the fort were now aware that a new weapon had been brought to bear against them. A few were brave enough to pop up from time to time, to try to hit the men working the catapult, but the low wall protected them.

One bundle of dynamite was not put into the basket firmly enough. It fell out, onto the ground next to the catapult. One of the miners leaped forward and tore the fuse loose. After that, they were more careful.

Finally, a load of dynamite was dropped right into the fort. The miners could hear excited yelling, doors slamming, then a blast lifted some debris high up above the log walls.

"Why doesn't Jennings give up?" Peterson wondered aloud, looking worriedly at the fort. "It's gotta be soon. Eventually, it's going to get dark."

"Probably exactly what Jennings is thinking," Gabe replied.

He decided to help matters along. Taking his Sharps, he climbed to the top of the hose tower. The lookout was still there. He made room for Gabe, glad to have company. "Boy, that dynamite's sure got 'em runnin'," the lookout said, grinning.

Gabe nodded. He took off his duster and laid it on the ledge of a small window that looked in the direction of the fort. Two hundred yards. An easy shot with the Sharps. He'd often used it to shoot a buffalo at five hundred yards.

Gabe flipped open the rifle's chamber. It was an old rifle, originally it had been designed for powder, ball, and a percussion cap, but he'd had it modified to take metal cartridges. The rifle had been given to him years before by the old mountain man, Jim Bridger. Right after Bridger had gotten him out of the army guardhouse. Right after Gabe had broken his trigger finger on that captain's jaw.

At one time, he'd hated Bridger, who'd kidnapped him from his mother's tipi when Gabe was a boy—with his mother's cooperation—then taken him to that damned army fort, to learn to live among the whites. It had taken Gabe a long time to accept the fact that both of them thought they were doing it for his own good. Well, maybe it actually had been for the best; he'd learned enough about the whites to know how to keep them from killing him.

Gabe slipped one of the Sharps's huge cartridges into the chamber. He'd loaded the cartridges himself, weighing out each load, seating the bullet carefully, so each would fire exactly like all the others.

He raised the rear sight, set it for two hundred yards. Then he cranked back the hammer. Laying the rifle's fore stock on his rolled up duster, muzzle pointed toward the fort, he settled down to wait.

He could see most of the courtyard. Little was moving down there. The dynamite attack—although little of the dynamite had actually fallen inside the fort itself—was forcing everyone to lie low. Then Gabe saw movement in one of the barracks windows. The dynamite had blown out the glass, and he could see faces close to the opening, peering out. He pulled on the set trigger then transferred the bent tip of his index finger to the main trigger. An easy shot. He fired almost offhand, sending a bullet smashing into the window's wooden frame. Splinters flew, and the faces vanished from the window.

After that he fired slowly, sending bullets through every opening. And through the roofs, knowing they were thin. He could see the roof of Jennings's office, but not the door, which was on the far side of the office. Gabe put three rounds through the roof before he heard the door crash open, then saw Jennings come running out, holding onto his hat, sprinting for the barracks. Gabe managed to reload in time to get off one more shot before Jennings disappeared into the barracks. But not a shot designed to kill; he wanted to wait for that, wait until he could look Jennings straight in the eye. But he did manage to pepper Jennings with splinters from the door frame. He smiled when he saw Jennings clutch at his side.

The catapult was working again. Gabe saw a package of dynamite drop into the courtyard. But it did not explode. Perhaps the fuse had gone out as the dynamite rushed through the air. Gabe fired at it, but missed by a couple of inches. While he was reloading, a man ran out of the barracks and picked up the dynamite, then rushed back inside before Gabe could fire again.

The day dragged on. At three o'clock, Peterson called out for Jennings to surrender. His only answer was a blast of fire from a rifle. Whoever was shooting was out of Gabe's view.

The shadows grew longer. Bored with his potshotting, Gabe climbed down from the tower. Making his way opposite the fort's front gate, he saw that Peterson was looking worried. "It'll be dark soon," Peterson grumbled. "I'm sure the bastard is gonna make his move sometime tonight."

"Maybe not," Gabe said. "Maybe he figures somebody will miss him. Send help."

Peterson shook his head. "Uh-uh. I've already let him know that we're sending out regular business via the telegraph. It'll be days before somebody begins to wonder."

Gabe nodded. "You'll just have to make sure the men stay alert tonight. And tomorrow night, and the night after. However long it takes."

Gabe took hold of Peterson's arm and forced Peterson to face him. "Jennings," Gabe said, his voice hard now, "he's mine. I want you to remember that."

Peterson seemed mesmerized by the cold light in Gabe's eyes. "Sure," he said. "Sure. You've done a lot for us. You certainly deserve at least that much." But Peterson, new to violence, was disturbed by Gabe's intensity.

Night fell. Gabe and Peterson made the rounds, keeping the guards on their toes. Most of their little force was right in front of the gates. A few were posted around the back and sides, but not many, because, if the gunmen tried to go out over the walls, they would be easy targets. And they'd have to leave on foot.

Halfway through the night, a man came up to Peterson. "Johnson," Peterson snapped, "how come you've left your post?"

Johnson seemed annoyed at being addressed like a private. "Goddamn it, Peterson, I just wanted to tell ya—over on our side, we been hearin' 'em diggin'. Maybe they're tryin' to tunnel out."

Peterson thought for a moment. "That doesn't make any sense," he finally said. "Where the hell would they be tunneling to?"

"Well," Johnson said sourly, "just thought you oughta know."

Gabe had been catnapping several yards away. He finally became aware of what the man was saying. Getting up, he asked him to repeat himself. "How long have you been hearing digging?" he asked.

"Oh, a coupla hours."

Gabe turned toward Peterson. "We have to get some men over to that side, fast. I think they're going to—"

Suddenly there was a tremendous blast from the far side of the fort. Gabe remembered the dynamite that had fallen into the fort, but failed to explode. Perhaps Jennings had had even more dynamite to augment the unexploded package the man had picked up. Gabe had a mental image of Jennings's men, digging a hole beneath the foundations of one of the fort's walls, then filling that hole with dynamite.

Gabe, Peterson, and a dozen other men raced toward the far side of the fort. Smoke and dust were rising into the air. Gabe saw that a huge gap had been blown through the log walls. The dust was still settling when a stream of horsemen poured through the gap, heading for the far edge of town, riding right past the two men whom Johnson had left guarding that wall, men who were still too stunned from the blast to use their rifles. "Goddamn!" Gabe heard Peterson shout. "The bastard's gone and done it! He's busted out!"

CHAPTER FOURTEEN

Men were running in every direction. Peterson was kicking at the ground, his face working angrily. "He'll be out there," he muttered. "He can sweep back in anytime, hit us when we don't expect it."

"That's why we have to go after him," Gabe said. "Now. Before he can get set."

Peterson turned toward Gabe. His eyebrows rose. "We don't know where he's going."

"We can follow him."

"In the dark?" Peterson asked dubiously.

"Yes, in the dark. As long as we get on his trail right away."

"You really think you can follow him?" Peterson asked, scratching his chin. "Because I'm damned sure none of us could."

"Like I said, as long as we get moving right away."

Peterson kept looking at Gabe, still scratching his chin. "Yeah," he finally said. "I suppose if anybody could do it, it'd be you."

Within fifteen minutes, Gabe and Peterson had gathered twenty men. They set off at once. Gabe found it relatively easy to follow Jennings's trail; he and his men had rushed off so wildly that they'd left a highway of sign behind them. Once or twice, when the trail branched, Gabe had to spend time checking out each route, making certain that Jennings wasn't leaving false sign in an attempt to mislead anyone tracking him.

It soon became clear to Gabe that Jennings wasn't making any attempt at all to cover his tracks. Gabe took that as evidence of Jennings's contempt for the miners.

Three hours after starting out, Gabe saw the glow of a campfire, about a mile ahead. He asked Peterson to halt the men. "Only one or two of us should go on from here," Gabe said.

"Why?" Peterson asked. "Now that we know where they are . . ."

"Do you really want to tangle with the kind of men Jennings has?" Gabe asked. "In the dark?"

Peterson allowed as how he hadn't really thought of it that way. Gabe finally set off, taking only one other man with him, a middle-aged miner who had once been a trapper. He gave the impression of knowing how to move in the wilderness.

Gabe and the old trapper, whose name was Stanley, rode forward another half mile, then dismounted. They covered the rest of the distance on foot. The last two hundred yards required over an hour of careful stalking, moving from one dark mass of cover to the next. Finally, they were in place, only about fifty yards from the campfire.

Jennings and his men obviously believed they were safe; their horses were unsaddled and staked out some ways from the campsite. The men themselves were lying at their ease on their bedrolls around the fire.

Gabe immediately spotted Jennings striding back and forth in front of the fire. He was the only man on his feet. He had a bottle in one hand. Every few steps, he put the bottle to his lips and tilted his head back.

While Gabe and Stanley had been making their approach, they'd been aware that an argument was going on among the men. The closer they got, the easier it was to understand the actual words. Apparently, the argument had to do with their next move. "What the hell's the matter with you boys?" Jennings was saying. "Lost your guts? I say we go back in the morning, just ride in and shoot the hell out of those goddamned miners."

"We wasn't shootin' the hell out of 'em when we left," one man replied acidly. Gabe saw that it was the man who'd been sitting on his bunk while Gabe had collected his gear. Apparently, he hadn't been able to make it out in time. "Hell," the man continued, "now they even got the fort to hole up in."

"Maybe we could just kinda make things hot for 'em," another man said. Gabe saw that it was Ace. "You know . . . pick one or two of 'em off now and then. Make 'em nervous."

"Play cowboys and Indians?" Jennings jeered. "Uh-uh. When we go back there, we go in style. Ride right in and put the fear of God into Peterson and his damn gophers. No goddamn buncha workin' stiffs is gonna make me sneak through the brush."

"Well," one man said. "They ain't all miners. There's that bastard Conrad. He'll be helpin' 'em out. Showin' 'em how to—"

"Bullshit!" Jennings snapped. "Conrad'll be long gone. He's got nothin' in common with the miners. They got nobody except Peterson, and he's not a fighting man."

"Conrad sure as hell was helpin' 'em when they had us pinned down in the fort," the man replied.

"Yeah," Jennings said. "That's because he's after me. But with us long gone . . ."

"Hell, maybe he's on our trail right now."

"Shit, who cares?" Jennings shot back. "There's not much one man can do on his own. No, I say we rest up a few hours, then ride back at dawn, hit 'em hard when they don't expect it. If we do a good job, I promise there'll be a big bonus in it for every man jack here."

There was a murmur of approval from the men. Except for one, the man who had told Gabe in the barracks that he was leaving. He stood up now. "Well," he drawled, "you boys go on and get yourselves all shot up. I'm pullin' up stakes right now. Ridin' on, lookin' for a healthier way to make a livin'."

He looked around at the others. "Anybody else want to ride along?"

Some of the men stirred . . . until Jennings interrupted. He threw the bottle into the fire, which flared up as some of the alcohol sprayed into the flames. He turned toward the man who'd just spoken. "You ain't goin' nowheres, Jones," he said, his voice harsh. "You signed on to do a piece o' work. You were glad to take the money when it was easy goin', but now that the chips are down, you want to run out on us."

"You can think what you want, Jennings," Jones said. "I happen to think this whole thing's too screwed up to pull outta the fire. You just wanta stay in good with the money boys back East. Me, I think I'll head on out to California."

Jones turned, probably to head for his horse. Perhaps some of the other men might have followed him, but Jennings pulled out his pistol, cocked it, and shot Jones in the back.

"Jesus!" one man said, twisting out of the way as Jones fell next to him.

Jennings stood, backlit by the fire, his pistol still in his hand, a lazy trail of smoke rising from the muzzle. "Anybody else got a hankerin' for California?" he asked, his voice cold as ice.

No one moved, or spoke. There were still over a dozen gunmen. Together, they could easily take Jennings. But not a one among them wanted to be the first to try. Gabe, watching, was beginning to realize just what it was that allowed Jennings to control these hard, dangerous men. He was crazy mean. He had no fear at all.

Jennings scanned each man, one by one. Finally, he holstered his pistol. "It's settled, then. We ride out a little before dawn."

Most of the men nodded. Some were silent, but they did not dispute Jennings's decision. "Get that garbage outta here," Jennings said, pointing toward Jones's body. Two men leapt up and dragged Jones back into the brush.

Once again, the gunmen were showing signs of being a well-organized force. Gabe watched as Jennings posted guards for the night. He wondered why it had not been done before, then he smiled. Maybe the one man's comment that Gabe might be on their trail had gotten Jennings thinking again, planning around his usual alcoholic fog.

Gabe slid closer to Stanley and whispered in his ear, "Go on back to Peterson. Tell him that in an hour or so he should start moving the men up onto the high ground overlooking the campsite . . . that little hill right over there. We have enough guns to surround Jennings. As long as it's done quietly."

Stanley nodded, then quickly crawled away. Gabe remained behind, watching the camp. Everyone was settling down, hoping to get some sleep before the morning's action. Half an hour later, even from fifty yards away, Gabe could hear snores. But Jennings was still on his feet, once again pacing by the fire. How it must have galled him to be chased out of his own fort. If he did manage to retake the town, there would be a lot of killing.

Jennings was drinking again. How can the man stay on his feet with all that alcohol in him? Gabe wondered. Finally, growing tired, Jennings growled at a guard, then lay down.

Gabe had been growing very interested in the guards. One was patrolling the area where the horses were tied. The other was making a slow circuit of the camp's perimeter. Neither appeared very alert. That decided Gabe. Even with the miners outnumbering the gunmen, Gabe still didn't know how easy it would be to take them. However, if he could break the gunmen's morale . . .

It took Gabe another half hour to reach a spot where he could intercept the perimeter guard. Finally as the man walked past, Gabe rose up behind him, hit him on the head with his pistol butt, then grabbed him before he could fall, clamping his hand over his mouth to stifle any cry of pain.

Gabe lay beside the unconscious man for a full minute, listening for indications that anyone had been alerted. Nothing but snores. He slowly dragged the man away. When he figured he was far enough from the camp, Gabe bound and gagged the man, leaving him hidden in a clump of brush. It would have been easier to kill him, but perhaps the gunmen would be even more demoralized when they discovered that whoever had raided them hadn't thought it necessary.

Now the horses. Gabe smiled. No one was as good at stealing horses as a Lakota. Not the Crow, not the Pawnee, not even the Cheyenne. Well, maybe the Apache. Gabe had been stealing horses since he was a boy. He remembered the raids he had made with his fellow Oglala warriors, the tension as they stole up on a camp of their old enemies, the Crow. The exhilaration as they rode away with Crow horses. What a wonderful life that had been! Of course, the Crow would have killed them if they'd been caught, which made their triumph all the more exciting.

Tonight was like playing games with children. Ten minutes later the horse guard was unconscious, bound and gagged. The hard part was keeping the horses from growing nervous as Gabe moved among them, carefully cutting lead ropes. It was even more dangerous to get the horses moving. Fortunately the lead ropes were long, and the horses had been tethered too far from the camp.

The night was almost over. In a little while Jennings's camp would wake up . . . to find that things were going very wrong. Gabe, once he was further away, moved as quickly as possible, with the horses jostling and grumbling along behind him. He took them way around to one side, behind the hill where he had told Stanley to have Peterson post the men.

A jumpy miner almost shot Gabe. "Jesus!" the guard hissed, finally lowering the hammer of this rifle. "With all those horses, I thought you was . . ."

Gabe left the horses with the guard, then went up the rear slope of the hill. Peterson was delighted to see him. Even more delighted to discover that Jennings now had no mounts.

"Everybody in place?" Gabe asked.

"Yes," Peterson replied. "It was real thoughtful of Jennings's boys to light that fire for us. Otherwise, we might have gotten lost. Oh, here," he added. "We brought this along for you."

Peterson handed Gabe his Sharps carbine. A cautious check, careful to avoid noise, showed Gabe that it was loaded. He looked up and realized that it was light enough to see the grin on Peterson's face. Already, he could hear someone stirring below in Jennings's camp. Gabe looked along the hilltop. Men were posted behind every rock. The camp lay only about sixty yards away, below the hill. A bluff on the far side would make it difficult for the gunmen to slip away. "They're yours," Gabe said to Peterson. "Any way you want them."

"I want them alive," Peterson said. "If there's a lot of killing, we'll hang. Oh, by the way. I hear that one of the foremen, Heerden, was killed in a cave-in, along with four miners. Too bad. Terrible accident."

Gabe nodded. So he would not be called to account for Heerden's death. It was Peterson's way of telling him that it would pay to keep things calm. A shame. With Jennings this close . . .

Gabe could hear someone calling out inside the camp. "Ben? Where the hell are you? Ben?"

Probably someone calling for one of the missing guards. Now other men were waking up. "What the hell you yappin' about?" someone asked. It sounded like Jennings.

"Ben. He's supposed to be walking perimeter. I don't see hide nor hair of him."

A curse. Now Gabe was sure it was Jennings. "If that son of a bitch lit out during the night . . . Get over to the horses. See if his nag is still there."

There was more cursing, then a short time later, a cry, coming from the far side of the camp. "Hell, boss! There ain't no horses at all! An' Jackson's all tied up!"

It was light now, light enough to make out everyone in the camp. Gabe saw Jennings jump to his feet. "Damn!" Jennings snarled. He looked around wildly. In another moment, he'd act.

Gabe signaled to the miners. The loading levers of thirty rifles were slammed forward and back, a sound that racketed in the ears of the men below.

"Don't any one of you make a move!" Peterson called out.

The gunmen, not quite sure how bad the situation might be, froze in place. All except for one man. Perhaps he was still groggy with sleep, too groggy to realize the hopelessness of their position. He picked up a rifle and started to aim it up at the hill. Gabe aimed briefly with the Sharps and pulled the trigger. The heavy boom of the big gun reverberated through the hills. Squinting past a huge cloud of white powder smoke, Gabe saw the gunman fly backward as the huge slug took him square in the chest. After the man hit the ground, he never even twitched.

With this rather graphic example of the futility of resistance planted firmly in their minds, the rest of the gunmen held perfectly still. A few slowly raised their hands; they had no idea how many men had the drop on them. But from the sounds of all those rifles cocking, it had to be a hell of a lot.

Jennings was standing, hands on his hips, looking down at the ground. He was the only one among them who looked relaxed, except for the rhythmic tapping of one toe against the ground. He wants to kill, Gabe thought.

Peterson called out, "Every one of you toss your weapons over toward that big rock."

Nothing happened, so Peterson fired straight into the campfire. Sparks and chunks of burning wood flew. "Now!" he shouted.

The time for the gunmen to make their move had already passed. If they'd resisted immediately, some of them might have escaped. Gabe saw one man shrug, then toss his pistol away from him. Others followed. Soon every one of them was disarmed. Peterson sent four men down to collect the weapons.

Jennings had been the last man to disarm himself. Head down, he glared from under his eyebrows up at the hill. He had not said a word.

Peterson came down from the hill, backed up by four riflemen. He swept his gaze over the gunmen. "We could have killed you," he said. "You know that. But that's not the way we work. We've got your guns and your horses. You can have the horses back—you'll need them to ride the hell out of here. Just make sure you ride good and far. Because, if any of you head back this way ever . . . you'll be killed on sight."

The horses were brought out from behind the hill. Peterson gave the gunmen ten minutes to pack up their gear—minus their guns—then ordered them to mount. "Now ride," he said. "And keep riding."

Jennings mounted with his men. Gabe had come down from the hill and now stood alongside Peterson. Jennings looked from one to the other. Finally, he spoke. "You made a big mistake," he said tightly. "Not killing us."

Peterson met his gaze squarely. "That can be rectified," he snapped. "Right now."

Gabe decided that Peterson meant it. So did Jennings. His gaze dropped. He turned his horse, started away. But he could not resist one last glance back over his shoulder. His eyes locked onto Gabe. "You're a dead man, Conrad!" he shouted, then put spurs to his horse.

CHAPTER FIFTEEN

During the trip back to town, Gabe rode a little apart from the others, lost in thought. How different the White Man's way appeared. In some ways they were too soft, in others, more ruthless than wolverines. He knew, as a Lakota, that it was very dangerous to leave an enemy alive. Particularly after humiliating him the way Jennings had been humiliated. A beaten but living enemy was always a danger. Not only to oneself, but to those a man held close.

Like Gabe's mother. And his wife. He had let Captain Stanley Price live, after the fight during which Gabe had broken his finger on the captain's jaw. At the end of the fight, Gabe had been standing over the captain with a pitchfork raised high, ready to end it as it should have been ended. With Price dead.

It was Jim Bridger who stopped him from thrusting down with the pitchfork. Ironically, Bridger had originally kept Price's fellow officers from killing Gabe, had covered them with his Sharps, the same one Gabe carried now, while he and Price fought. Bridger had turned that same Sharps onto Gabe when Gabe was about to finish Price. Bridger had forced him to let Price live.

Even though he'd been only a boy, not quite twenty, Gabe had known that it was a mistake. But how could he have known that it was his loved ones who would pay for that mistake, rather than himself?

As Gabe rode along with the triumphant miners, images began to flood his mind. Horrifying memories. Of Yellow Buckskin Girl, his new wife, his beautiful wife, his love. Of Yellow Buckskin Girl, already with one bullet in her abdomen, being shot in the forehead by Captain Stanley Price, that day the army had raided the village. Of Yellow Buckskin Girl falling dead, and a moment later, Price, after glaring triumphantly in Gabe's direction, thrusting his saber through Gabe's mother's breast. Gabe still remembered the terrible look of agony and shock on his mother's face.

Worst of all, the horror of being unable to do anything to stop what was happening. At that moment, Gabe had a terrified baby under each arm, trying to save them from the soldiers, who were killing men, women, and children. Even the camp dogs.

Later, the sadness, the grieving. He had laid Yellow Buckskin Girl's body on a raised platform, in the Lakota manner. But he had dug a grave for his mother and laid her in it, knowing that was what she as a white woman would want. All that grief, as he said good-bye to the two women he loved so much. He still bore scars on his arms and chest, thin white lines, where he had slashed himself to show his agony.

And all because he had left an enemy alive. Of course, Stanley Price had paid. Paid horribly. Gabe had hunted him down, shot his way through Price's bodyguards, pursued him across a snowy landscape. There was another image. Price, running out of a burning barn, his body a ball of flame. A death he deserved. But it had not brought back Amelia Conrad nor Yellow Buckskin Girl. Because Gabe had let an enemy live. And this man, this Jennings, he was the kind of man who would live for vengeance. At least there was no one here close to Gabe for Jennings to kill. Just Gabe himself.

Once back in town, Gabe took a room at the town's only hotel. Peterson wanted him to join in with the others, celebrating Jennings's rout, but Gabe wanted time to himself. Time to think, time to decide what he wanted to do next. He'd already considered riding off into the mountains, but he suspected that he was not yet finished in this place. Something was holding him. Perhaps it was Taffy's spirit, roaming, lost and angry, down in the mine. Inside the Devil's Guts, as Taffy always called it.

Gabe ended up sleeping most of the day away. A knock on the door woke him up late in the afternoon. Still a little groggy, Gabe rolled out of bed, picked up one of his pistols, and moved to the side of the door. Instinctive behavior. Particularly after the past few weeks.

One of the miners was at the door. The man had his hat in his hands. "Just wanted to let you know that they're gonna bury Taffy and his mates in a little while. Maybe you'd like to . . ."

Gabe nodded, started to turn away. The man held up a hand. "An' I just wanted to let you know," he said, a little shyly, "we *all* want you to know, how we appreciate what you been doin' for us."

Then the man was gone. Gabe picked up a pitcher, poured water into a basin, and washed his face and arms. Then he strapped on his guns and left the room.

The burial was muted; there was no preacher. Gabe watched as they laid Taffy and the three men from his crew into a damp, clayey hole in the ground. Taffy had traveled a long way to die. Watching him disappear into his grave, Gabe felt confused. He had no further business here. He should ride on. But Taffy, and most of the other miners, had been struggling toward something they considered important enough to risk their lives for. The survivors thought they had finally won, but Gabe knew better. The men who owned the mine would not let the miners keep their triumph. The whole might of the state would be behind the owners. The Republican party held power, had held it for a long time. The party of Lincoln

had become the party of big business. It would not permit
workingmen to stand up for their rights. Immense force would
be brought against them. They had little chance of prevailing.
Many would die. Standing by them would be dangerous.

This is not my fight, Gabe told himself. This is more of
the White Man's foolishness, another manifestation of his
unlimited greed. Ride on, he warned himself. But then, there
was Taffy. His courage, his hopes and dreams.

Gabe knew that he could not think inside a town. He had to
feel the land around him, look up at a sky clear of filth from
smokestacks, be near a stream of clear water, hear nothing
but the sighing of the wind, the song of birds, the sounds of
animals.

He went back up to his room, packed his gear, then, coming
downstairs, strapped it onto his horse. Mounting, he headed out
of town. Along the way he caught sight of Peterson, talking to
a group of men. Peterson looked up as Gabe passed, but said
nothing, did not call out for him to stay. The man watched
him calmly. Gabe suspected that Peterson would only want
him to do what Gabe himself thought right.

Gabe rode straight to the meadow where he'd stayed before
he'd decided to work for Jennings. It was dark when he arrived,
but he knew the place, had held it in his memory during the time
he was a prisoner down inside the mine. After taking care of
his horse, he lay out his bedroll, undressed, and lay down. He
was hungry, but had no intention of eating. He would not eat
until he had done what he had come here to do.

The next morning Gabe woke with the sun. He rolled
out of his bedroll and stood naked in the cool morning
air. How heavy he felt, how loaded down with dross. His
whole being had been dirtied by the events of the past
weeks. The time he'd spent with Jennings and his gunmen. The horror of the mine. He needed to be clean again.

But washing in the little stream would not be enough. He
needed washing inside as well as outside; he needed to cleanse
his spirit. He needed *inipi*.

Naked, he roamed the area, looking for stones, not just any stones, but stones of the right kind. Within ten minutes he had found a dozen, each about four or five inches thick, stones that would neither explode nor crumble when they grew hot.

Next he began to gather wood, dry wood that would not smoke, but would give off great heat. Bringing the wood back to his campsite, he laid down four good-sized pieces, stacking them so that they pointed east and west, then he stacked four more on top of the first four, pointing north and south. The stones he had collected went on top of the wood. Using kindling, he set fire to the wood. He waited until the fire was burning well, licking up past the stones. Picking up his knife, he went down to the stream where he cut twelve thin willow saplings, each taller than himself. He brought the saplings back to the fire.

The fire was burning well; he could feel heat beginning to radiate from the stones. Now it was time to build the lodge. After carefully choosing a spot not too far from the fire, a spot with the right kind of feeling, Gabe used his knife to dig a dozen small holes, forming a circle about seven feet across. Next, he peeled the bark from the saplings, then stuck the bigger end of each sapling into one of the holes, tamping down the earth until they were firmly held in place. He then dug a shallow pit in the center of the circle.

Next, he bent the saplings inward, using strips of bark to tie them in place, until he had formed the skeleton of a small dome about four feet high. Satisfied, he scouted the area, collecting several clumps of sage. He spread some of the sage on the ground inside the dome at the north side, where it would form a comfortable place to sit. Other bundles of sage were stacked loosely near the first bundle, where they would be easy to reach.

Now the dome would have to be covered. Animal skins would have been best, but he did not have any. On his way out of town, he had stopped to pick up a length of canvas, which he now draped over the frame. The framework was covered, except for a section at one side, which he would use as a door.

He unrolled his heavy buffalo-hide coat and draped it over the entrance. Now the sweat lodge was completely enclosed.

He went over to the fire. The stones were glowing with an almost white heat. Cutting a pair of forked sticks, he used them as tongs to carry the stones one by one into the sweat lodge, where he arranged them in a sacred pattern in the central pit. He also carried a few coals inside and put them on top of the rocks, then moved some of the sage close to the pit. His canteen went next to the sage.

Going outside once again, he stood for a moment, aware of how good the sun felt on his naked body. Then, picking up his pipe and smoking mixture, he crawled into the sweat lodge, pulling the flap closed behind him. He skirted the central pit. His skin cringed at the heat coming from the rocks. He seated himself facing the central pit on the cushion of sage he had laid down.

It took a while for his eyes to adjust to the darkness. There was a little light coming from the coals on top of the rocks and a little more from poorly sealed joints in the sweat lodge covering. Finally, he filled and lit the pipe, performing the usual ritual. The smoke felt good going into him. After he had smoked, he threw some of the sage onto the fire. It began to burn, and he inhaled its aromatic smoke.

A few minutes later the coals winked out, leaving only the dark red glow of the hot stones. He poured a little water over his head and face, then, using a crude dipper he had made out of twigs, he sprinkled water over the stones. The water hissed and spat, and steam immediately began to fill the sweat lodge.

He put water on the stones four times in all. The second time, there was a sharp report, like a rifle shot. One of the stones had split. The steam became thicker, hot, feeling alive as it pressed in on him. Breathing was difficult. The steam seared his throat. Sweat poured from his face and body. His eyes stung. He could not see. The smell of burning sage coated his tongue. The urge to escape, to go outside into the clean cool air, was very powerful.

But Gabe remained seated, chanting sacred songs, songs to *Wakan-tanka*, whom the White Man called the Great Spirit. Songs of communication, supplication. A request for strength, clarity of mind.

As the steam diminished, Gabe sprinkled water on the stones for the third time. There was less of an effect—the stones were cooling—but still there was steam, clouds of searing, purifying steam.

When he sprinkled water on the stones for the fourth and last time, he experienced a feeling of peace, well-being, suffusing his person, his mind, his body. The dross, the ugliness of the past few weeks, had been purged from him.

It was time now, it was enough. Gabe gathered up his canteen and pipe and crawled from the lodge out into the open. The air felt wonderful against his sweaty skin. He ran to the stream, plunged in, gasped at the water's coolness. He lay quietly in the water, letting it flow over him, washing away the sweat. He was once again complete. His *ni* had been restored. Now, each breath he took filled him with strength, with that boundless energy that existed throughout the whole of existence, that mysterious force that made up the entirety of all that was.

Gabe laughed with pleasure. He had lived many years among the white men, he'd learned their ways. He'd been reading his mother's Bible since boyhood, and he found much good in it. He knew what the White Man's world had to offer, but in all his years in the white world, he'd never yet found, among all the different white beliefs, anything that had more to offer than those things he'd learned as a boy, growing up among the Lakota. The way of oneness with the earth and sky and wind and water. The way of completeness.

Gabe began pulling apart the sweat lodge, throwing the willow saplings into the brush. He brought water from the stream and poured it over the stones until they were cool enough to remove. He tossed them into the stream. Lashing the canvas into a bundle, he tied it behind his saddle, over his bedroll.

Then he dressed. But when he was fully dressed with his guns in place, he laid aside his duster, with its torn right side stained with blood, and picked up the heavy buffalo-hide coat. He spread the coat upon the grass, so that he could look at the design that spread across the coat's back . . . the stylized figure of a great bird, with its wings spread wide. *Wakinyan*, the Winged One. What the White Man called the Thunderbird. *Wakinyan*, who had come to him during his vision quest. . . .

When Gabe had come back to his people, after escaping from the fort after his fight with Captain Price, he had felt in need of a vision, something that would reveal to him where he now stood in the scheme of existence. The old Oglala medicine man, High Backbone, had instructed him as to what he must do. Gabe had gone to a high place, where he had fasted, sung, and prayed for four days. Finally, when he was at last certain that no vision would come to him, one had. A horrifying vision. Of his mother, lying dead, deep in the earth. Of himself, following a trail that led away from the People. And the People themselves, destroyed, their way of life gone forever.

But in the midst of these horrors, he had heard the sound of great wings beating above him, and *Wakinyan* had settled down onto Gabe, his wings folding over Gabe's shoulders, filling him with a sense of power and of being protected by a force greater than his own.

When he had later told his mother of his visitation by *Wakinyan*, she, having lived long enough with the Oglala to have become a little like them herself and proud of the honor shown her son in his vision, had painted a mighty figure of *Wakinyan* onto the side of a new tipi cover she was making. In bright colors, she painted the Winged One with his wings outspread.

A short time later that new tipi cover had been burned by the soldiers, with only charred remnants left. But one of those remnants held the complete figure of *Wakinyan*.

Taking this as a sign, Gabe had cut the figure clear of the ruined tipi cover and fashioned it into this coat. His war coat.

Now, standing in the meadow, his mind and body purged by *inipi*, Gabe put the coat on, and as it settled over his shoulders, he was once again aware of a feeling of power suffusing him, aware that the wings of *Wakinyan* were once again wrapped protectively around him.

He mounted and rode out of the meadow, a warrior on his way to war, because there would definitely be a war. But now he rode no longer as Gabe Conrad, but as Long Rider, Oglala warrior.

CHAPTER SIXTEEN

The next few days were days of entrenchment, a time for Peterson and his lieutenants to decide the best strategy for consolidating the miners' position. If there was one, single position. Because it was also a time of endless argument, of jockeying for power, of hot little pockets of self-interest.

Disgusted, Gabe kept pretty much to himself. However, considering his history in local events, he was noticed by many. Especially now, wearing the long buffalo-hide coat with the brightly colored Thunderbird on the back. One day an old miner came up to him. "That there coat reminds me of somethin' I once heard," the miner said. " 'Bout a feller got hisself in some trouble. Feller who called hisself Long Rider."

Getting no reaction from Gabe, the miner added hastily, "I don't mean nasty trouble. Just that this Long Rider feller took on some rich bastards, gave 'em a hard time. He wore the same kinda coat you got. Never met him myself, but I was jus' wonderin'. . . ."

Instead of answering, Gabe simply walked away. But he could hear the old miner's voice, behind him, beginning to regail his listeners. "This man I'm talkin' about . . . he ain't the kinda man you'd wanna piss off. Why, I heard about the time . . ."

Gabe walked on out of earshot. Long Rider. A name he seldom used in the White Man's world. His Oglala name. The name he had earned for himself when he was still little more than a boy.

When Gabe had been fourteen, word had come that a cavalry column was on its way, that its route would take it right through the territory of a neighboring group of Indians. In Gabe's village, most of the men were absent, out on a hunt. Gabe had been the one chosen to ride to the neighboring people with a warning that the soldiers were on the way. It was winter, a particularly severe winter. For several days Gabe rode through a howling blizzard, going through two horses. But he got through, and because of his epic ride, he was given the name Long Rider. A name he did not care to share with the white world. They knew him as Gabe Conrad, and to them he would remain Gabe Conrad.

Gabe spent most of his time with Peterson. He was impressed by the way the former lawyer was organizing this mob of individualists. If Crazy Horse had had an organizer like Peterson, the land would probably still be Lakota.

The telegraph line remained open, and over this line Peterson was attempting to negotiate with the owners back East. With little success. The owners were completely hostile; their only replies were threats. Get out of the mine or end up being hanged as pirates.

Violent arguments broke out among the men. Some were in favor of sabotaging the mine itself. Others wanted to keep working it and use the profits for themselves. Peterson was successful in getting the men to simply maintain the mine shafts and drifts, keeping them in good condition.

Peterson's main opponent was Hank, the loudmouthed man with the black beard whom Gabe had already run afoul of several times. Hank's agenda was simply Hank. He wanted power, for its own sake. To feed his ego. A group of miners, the more violent men, often those who drank the most and shouted the loudest, backed Hank. But the majority were still behind Peterson.

Hank was aware that Gabe was close to Peterson. Unable to move openly against Peterson himself, he decided to go after Gabe. One day, backed by half a dozen rowdies, Hank braced Gabe out on the boardwalk. Hank stepped out in front; the other men, because of the narrowness of the boardwalk, were grouped behind him.

"Conrad," Hank growled. "How do we know you ain't some kinda spy for the company? Every one of us remembers the way you sold your gun to Jennings. . . . Maybe you should get your ass outta here while you still got one."

Gabe stood for a moment, silently watching Hank. He was getting tired of all the White Man's games going on around him. He was also growing bored. Unless something interesting happened soon, he'd definitely be riding on, but not because some bag of bluster told him to. "Hank," he said softly, "if you're not out of my way in five seconds, I'm going to kill you."

Accustomed to the arguing and hot air of the past few days, Hank was, for a moment, unaffected. Until he found himself caught by the look in Gabe's eyes. A look of such cold clarity that he was positive that Gabe meant exactly what he'd just said.

An icy hand clutched at Hank's guts. One part of him wanted to stand his ground, but another part, the one that wanted to go on living, caused him to back up, then step out of the way as Gabe moved forward. A moment later he and his men were looking at the painted bird on the back of Gabe's coat.

"That son of a bitch," Hank murmured, once he was certain Gabe would not be able to hear him. "One o' these days I'm gonna . . ."

He became aware of the skeptical looks on the faces of the men who'd been backing him up. "Well, by God, anybody got any smart words?" he demanded.

The men shook their heads. They were all too afraid of Hank to voice their disgust. But not as afraid of Hank as Hank was afraid of Gabe. His fear and embarrassment only made Hank hate Gabe all the more.

Gabe paid no attention. If Hank bothered him again, he would simply kill him. But by now there were more serious things to worry about. Some of the telegraph operators along the line, workingmen like those in the mine, would, from time to time, risk their jobs by relaying information to the miners. One afternoon Peterson called a meeting of all the men. Standing on a platform, facing over a hundred miners, he waved a telegram. "Real news, boys," he called out. "And not very good news. The word is out . . . the owners are gonna try to crush us. There's a train on the way carrying a couple of hundred armed strikebreakers. They mean to do us in."

A good judge of timing, Peterson didn't try to interfere as shouting broke out among the listening crowd. He waited until a husky miner shouted up at him, "Well, shit, Peterson, what the hell are we gonna do?"

The crowd fell silent. Every man wanted to know the answer to that question. Every man wanted to know if Peterson had some magic tucked away up his sleeve. He disappointed them by telling the truth. "We can do one of two things," he said gravely. "We can cut and run, which is the prudent thing to do. . . ."

Peterson let a moment pass. The crowd was still silent, hanging on his words. "Or," Peterson bellowed, his voice rising, "we can stay here and fight the bastards!"

Once again, his timing was perfect. A roar of approval came from the crowd. "We'll give 'em hell, Peterson!" one man cried out, his voice heard clearly above the general shouting.

Standing near the rear of the crowd, Gabe gave a small nod of appreciation. Peterson really knew how to talk to men, how to channel their feelings. He was a natural politician. Gabe smiled, wondering if he'd still like Peterson if he ever got elected to public office. That was pretty unlikely, though. Peterson had little chance of living through this mess.

The next few days were a madhouse of wild activity. Some of the men, those not willing to put their life on the line for what looked like a losing cause, left the area. But others arrived, more than enough to make up the defections. These were men from other mines, from other work sites, attracted by the idea of a fight, a chance to strike a blow for their own self-respect. Not all the newcomers were accepted. Peterson insisted that all gunmen and adventure seekers leave. He kept only workingmen, those committed to fighting back, at least this once, against the establishment that had been squeezing the life out of them for so long.

Tactics were argued endlessly. A railroad spur line ran into the town, for shipping out ore and bringing in mining supplies. If a train full of strikebreakers was on the way, these were the rails they would use. Some of the men were in favor of holing up in the fort, which overlooked the spur line, and fighting the strikebreakers from there . . . until it was pointed out that they would just be trapping themselves. Forts were only useful if those besieged inside could expect help from powerful forces outside. No help would be coming for the miners.

Others wanted to tear up the tracks, then wait for the strikebreakers to come in on foot. While the arguments continued, Gabe saddled his horse, then rode out along the railway line, studying the terrain. Three miles outside town, a railroad bridge spanned a rugged gully. All of the land on the town side of the bridge was just as rugged as the gully, a broken terrain of hogbacks and washes, perfect cover for defense, while the terrain on the far side was more open. And thus, more difficult for an attacking force to fight from.

Gabe rode back into town, where he spent half an hour with Peterson and his lieutenants. When he told Peterson what he had in mind, Peterson smiled. "Of course," he said. "We have to think like miners. We have to do what we do best. And what we really know is digging holes and blowing things up."

There were bunkers full of dynamite all around the mining area. The miners now invaded those bunkers and took out case after case of dynamite, not to blast gold-bearing rock, but to use for fighting. Bottles and cans were filled with dynamite and scrap—crude grenades. Most importantly, the railroad bridge three miles out of town was wired up, mined, with the most experienced blasters placing the charges. Meanwhile, bunkers were dug or blasted into the earth all across the rugged heights that overlooked the railroad bridge and its gully. One old miner, looking over the crude revetments, scratched his head. "Goddamn if it don't remind me just a little bit o' the siege o' Vicksburg."

The old miner stood for several minutes, watching, then added, "Sure hope it don't last nowhere near that long."

CHAPTER SEVENTEEN

Gabe walked along the bottom of the gully, looking up at the bridge. The dynamite charges were dark lumps, fastened to the bridge's wooden uprights by strong twine. The powder men were finishing the last of the fuses, running them down the bridge's cross members. They were long fuses, joining together to form the main fuse, which was supposed to end in a bunch of boulders a little way from the bridge. A lot depended on that fuse. If it should fail . . .

Gabe looked up at the hogback that rose above the bridge and the gully a hundred yards away. Not much showed, unless you knew it was there. The trenches had been dug by miners who knew how to dig a neat hole. The dirt had been carted away, rather than thrown down the slope. Gabe could see the heads of some of the men as they walked back and forth inside the trenches. When the time came, those heads had better be low, or the whole damned ambush would be exposed.

Gabe heard a man's voice rise up into a drawn-out cry. He looked upward. A man was standing at the hogback's highest point, shouting, and waving his arms. Gabe could barely make out the words.

"The train!"

Gabe trotted over to the men who were wrapping the last few yards of the fuse. "They've been sighted," he said to the chief blaster, a grizzled old miner with a gray-flecked beard.

"Shit," the blaster muttered. "Shoulda got this show on the road a helluva lot earlier."

"Can you finish?" Gabe asked.

The blaster glanced back at the boulders, still some distance away. "Five more minutes. Won't be able to bury the fuse, though. Don't like buryin' fuse, anyhow. Too much chance o' messin' it up."

Gabe nodded, then walked away, heading for the hogback. He climbed rapidly, hauling himself up the steep slope by grabbing hold of bushes. He reached the lowest trench and dropped down inside. Miners were stationed up and down the length of the trench, all of them with rifles. They all looked at him, some nervously, their eyes wide, scared— they'd all heard the lookout's cry—others were grinning, showing flashes of teeth.

Gabe started up one of the laterals that led to the higher levels. He found Peterson in a trench near the top of the hogback. Peterson appeared neither nervous nor pleased. Just grim. "What's the word?" Gabe asked.

Peterson pointed toward the east. "That. Out there," he replied.

Gabe looked, saw a plume of black smoke, a moving plume, progressing along the route covered by the railroad tracks.

"That's probably them," Peterson continued. "The timing would be just about right, considering when they left their last stop."

Word had been coming over the telegraph lines, coded messages from telegraph operators willing to stick their necks out. The train carrying the strikebreakers had been monitored for the past few hundred miles. There was no doubt that it was on its way. And little doubt that the plume of smoke drawing nearer and nearer was that same train. There was only one place this particular set of rails led to. The mine.

Gabe looked down into the gully. The blasters were still working with the main fuse. They should have been finished by now. Something had probably gone wrong. If they'd only had more time . . .

The blasters finally reached the cover of the boulders, the fuse trailing behind them like a long thin snake. Gabe heard Peterson mutter, "If we only had some of those electric detonators."

But they didn't. The dynamite under the bridge was going to have to be set off by hand. It would be a delicate matter of timing, planning the blast for the moment when the train was right in the middle of the bridge. There was no more talk of keeping bloodshed down. They'd been informed there were more than a hundred strikebreakers on the train. Over a hundred armed men. The dynamited bridge would have to take out as many as possible before the shooting started.

The smoke was quite near now, puffing upward from behind a low hill. Peterson stood up and made one last attempt to pump up men who were not, by trade, fighters. "Remember!" he cried out. "Wait for the word before you start shooting. We gotta take 'em by surprise."

Heads were popping up all along the rows of trenches. Gabe recognized tension on most of those faces. The ones who had been grinning before were no longer grinning, not now, with their enemies so close. Gabe wondered if any of them would cut and run.

"One thing, boys," Peterson added. "We can thank God that those tightwad mine owners were too cheap to hire Pinkertons. Those yahoos heading our way are just cheap saloon scum."

A sigh of relief passed along the line. Nobody wanted to fight the Pinkerton Detective Agency's hired killers. They were for sale to any industrialist who could pay their price. A hefty price. The Pinkertons were the most effective strike-breakers in the country. Totally ruthless.

The smoke was very close to the edge of that distant hill now. Peterson was playing it tight. "Okay," he finally shouted.

"Everybody down! Out of sight!"

Heads vanished all up and down the lines of trenches. Peterson turned to Gabe. "Had to wait," he explained. "Don't want 'em hunkered down too long, losing their nerve."

"You should have been a general," Gabe said, smiling, meaning it. Peterson grinned self-consciously. "I'd have settled for being born rich."

The train's engine suddenly appeared around a bend. Gabe and Peterson, peering through bushes that had been left as cover, watched the coaches follow. There were not many coaches, but each one appeared to be packed with men. There were several livestock cars at the rear of the train, undoubtedly loaded with horses.

The train approached the bridge. Gabe looked down toward the boulders. If they were going to light the fuse, they'd better do it now. Suddenly, there was a flash of fire, then a line of thick white smoke rising into the air, racing toward the bridge, as the powder inside the fuse began to burn. Too damned much smoke. The blasters, always firing off their charges inside a dark mine, had not considered how smoke from the fuses would look in daylight.

Gabe saw the blasters run out from behind the boulders, heading for cover further from the bridge. A route had already been laid out for them so they would not be seen from the train. But one man tripped. He rolled down a small cut-bank, ending up out in the open. He scrambled back under cover, but not before the train's engineer had spotted him. And seen the smoke rising from the burning fuses.

The engineer slammed the engine's drive wheels into reverse. Gabe could see sparks flying as the wheels spun against the rails. The whole train was sliding now. The engineer let out a series of shrieking blasts on his whistle. Gabe saw brakemen, spaced along the train, struggling to stay on their feet as they applied brakes for individual cars.

At this point, there was a bend in the rails. The last car, a livestock car, with too much force against it, slowly toppled over, pulling the one in front of it half off the rails. Gabe could hear the screams of frightened and injured horses coming from inside both cars.

It was the derailment of the last car, acting as a giant anchoring brake, that saved the train. The engine shuddered to a stop just yards short of the bridge. The dynamite exploded. A vast fountain of debris rose up into the air, obscuring Gabe's view of the engine. Dirt, wood, and pieces of hot metal rained down, as far away as the trenches. They'd used one hell of a lot of dynamite.

When the air had cleared a little, it could be seen that the bridge was gone, blown completely away. But the train was still sitting on the tracks, upright except for the last two cars, when it should have been lying down in the gully, smashed to pieces. Men were beginning to pour out of the coaches, every one of them carrying a rifle. In the hush after the explosion, Gabe could clearly hear their cries of surprise and outrage.

Then Peterson stood up in the trench, clearly visible. "Okay, boys!" he shouted, pointing down toward the train. "Give 'em hell!"

Men rose up in their trenches and shoved their rifles over the edge. A ragged blast of fire rippled up and down the lines.

Down by the train, the strikebreakers were still milling around. Now some of them began to fall. Bullets were kicking up dirt all around them; the miners were not, in general, the best of shots. But enough of those bullets were hitting home. The strikebreakers began to run, some toward the gully; but from the heights, the gully was no cover at all, most of it was in easy view of the riflemen above.

The strikebreakers had little choice but to run back to the train. But it gave poor cover, since the train was pointing straight at the hogback; the miners could see all of one side of the train and most of the other. The strikebreakers had to hunker down partly under the train itself. No point in hiding inside, since bullets from above ripped right through the cars' ceilings.

Unfortunately for the miners, not that many of the strikebreakers had gone down. And now they were shooting back, raggedly at first, but the volume of their fire soon increased. Gabe saw a man further along the trench hit in the head. He flew backward, blood spraying into the air, a wordless cry torn from his throat. His companions looked at the fallen man in horror; half his skull had been blown away. Gabe wondered if this might break them, seeing the immediacy of death, seeing one of their own killed. They might turn and run.

But, working in the mines, these men had seen plenty of death. And below them were men who wanted to force them to return to the dangerous conditions that had killed so many of them. With a cry of rage, the men around the fallen miner opened up a withering fire on the strikebreakers.

Gabe glanced over at Peterson. He could see the worry on the other man's face. If the train had only been on the bridge when the dynamite exploded . . .

But it had not, and now there would be a hard fight. Gabe saw Peterson's face tighten with determination. There would be no quitting.

The strikebreakers were becoming more organized. One man was circulating among them, putting men into the best possible positions for returning fire. The distance was over a hundred and fifty yards. It was difficult to see the man's face under the brim of his hat, but Gabe recognized him anyway, recognized the way he moved, the nervous authority in his manner. It was Jennings. He was with the strikebreakers.

Apparently he was leading them. Gabe picked up his Sharps, cranked back the big hammer, and started to sight in on Jennings. He'd much rather take him face-to-face, but it was important to get him now, before he rallied his confused men.

Jennings's head settled just above the Sharps's front sight. Gabe squeezed the trigger, felt the stock slam back against his shoulder. But Jennings was already bending low, starting to duck under cover. The huge bullet went through the crown of his hat, whipping it from his head. Jennings stood back up for a moment, hatless, staring at the hogback, at the pall of gun smoke rising into the air above the trenches. Staring, Gabe felt, straight at him.

Then Jennings disappeared from sight, behind the end of a coach.

Gabe felt someone tugging at his shoulder. It was Peterson. "Well, what do you think?" Peterson asked. "Should we rush them?"

Gabe shook his head vigorously, "No. We have a strong position here. Let them come to us—if they have the guts for it. They may just turn around and leave. I doubt they expected this much resistance."

"They could send for reinforcements. . . ."

"How? They're cut off down there. They'd have to go for miles to find a telegraph line. Let's just keep up the pressure. Maybe they'll surrender. Their horses are trapped inside those cars. . . ."

Suddenly, there was activity near the rear of the train, a couple of dozen men, running for a shallow depression fifty yards away. A cheer went up from the miners.

"They're running, just like you said!" Peterson cried out.

"The hell they are!" Gabe shouted back. He had spotted Jennings among the running men. Jennings would never run, not this early in a battle. "Get em!" he cried out. "Don't let them make it to cover!"

Some of the miners tried shooting at the running men, but the strikebreakers still at the train were giving good covering fire. The trenches were being swept by lead. Gabe managed to get one shot off with the Sharps and saw a man fall.

Then Jennings and his group were out of sight, inside the little depression. "Why do you think they went there?" Peterson asked.

"Because they've got cover now, almost all the way to this ridge. See how that depression connects to that other little ridge? Then that low spot?"

"Yeah," Peterson replied. "They're trying to flank us, aren't they?"

"They can't really flank us," Gabe said. "But they can get close enough to rush us. Look! There goes another group!"

Another twenty or so men were racing for the depression. This time more of the miners were able to open fire. Two of the running men were cut down, but the rest of them made it to cover. There were now at least thirty men hiding out of sight.

The firing died down a little. From time to time Gabe could see movement along the route he believed Jennings and his men would take. But it was difficult to get a good shot at them. "Tell the men," Gabe said to Peterson, "to get their explosives ready. But make sure Jennings's men don't hear you."

The word went along the trenches. Men stacked bottles and cans full of dynamite and scrap close at hand. Slow matches were lit, sending up little curls of blue smoke.

Suddenly at least two dozen men came racing from their final cover, right below the hogback. It was difficult for the miners to shoot down at them without rising up far enough to make a good target for the strikebreakers next to the train. Gabe saw a couple of Jennings's assault crew fall, then they were clawing their way up the hogback, while at the same time another twenty men made a sortie from the train.

In the trenches, the sound of shooting died down. When firing downhill, particularly at such a steep angle, it was easy to shoot high. But now a new sound engulfed the battlefield; the roar of explosions. One by one the crude handmade grenades were lit, then tossed or rolled down the slope. The ones filled with scrap and rock were the most devastating, literally blowing a few of the strikebreakers to pieces. Howling with fear, some of the attackers started to turn tail, to run . . . until Jennings shot one in the back.

"Up the goddamned hill!" he shouted. "Keep on climbing! Get right in among 'em! It's our only chance!"

A wedge of strikebreakers broke into the lowest trench. Encouraged, more of them raced from cover, intent on exploiting their new advantage. From above, Gabe and Peterson saw a milling mass of men struggling together. "I'm going down there!" Gabe shouted. "Our men need help!"

He raced down lateral trenches, heading for the fighting. He stopped just short of the lowest trench. From a position slightly above, he found himself looking down at a scene of desperate hand-to-hand fighting . . . pistols going off inches from faces, knives slashing, men strangling one another. Gabe pulled both his Colts from their holsters and began firing, carefully picking his targets, dropping a number of men. When the Colts were empty, he picked up a pick handle that had been dropped by a wounded miner and jumped down into the trench, swinging hard, cracking one man's skull, breaking another man's arm when he raised it to ward off the pick handle.

Gabe's arrival heartened the miners. They rallied, began to push the strikebreakers back. All except for one man. Hank. Gabe had already noticed Hank, lying on the floor of the tunnel, apparently dead or wounded. But now that the pressure had lessened a little, Hank got to his feet, apparently unhurt. He'd been playing possum. Blinking, eyes huge with fear, Hank spent a few seconds making certain that the fighting had moved away from him, then, with an inarticulate cry of fear, he turned and ran up the lateral, away from the enemy.

His cowardice immediately affected the other miners, who, aware of his panic, wondered if they were being hit from some new direction. They began to waver again. Sensing this, Jennings bellowed to his men, "Come on! We've got 'em running!"

Which might have happened . . . if Peterson had not shown up at that moment, along with a dozen reinforcements. This new force roared into the trench, shooting, screaming, giving heart to the besieged miners. Now it was the strikebreakers' turn to lose courage. Some began to turn and run, despite Jennings's desperate attempts to get them to hold fast. By now, Gabe and Jennings were only a few yards apart. Their eyes met and locked. If their guns had not been empty, they would have opened fire on one another. A tangled knot of struggling men separated them, yet each strained forward, eager to get at his enemy.

But it was not to be. The strikebreakers were falling back, some running as fast as they could. To stay would have cost Jennings his life; any of the miners would have been happy to kill him. Even so, he was one of the last to leave the trench, his eyes locking with Gabe's one last time, his lips moving, Gabe unable to hear the words, but knowing they formed a fatal promise.

Some of the miners were rash enough to try to chase the running strikebreakers across open ground . . . until a blast of fire from the other strikebreakers at the train drove them back. The two opposing sides were once again separated, the situation returning to what it had been before, with the exception of the growing number of dead and wounded.

A lull now fell over the battlefield, broken by an occasional random shot. Gabe and Peterson left the lower trenches and worked their way back up to their observation point. There, they found Hank, being held prisoner by half a dozen angry men. "Goddamned coward!" one miner was screaming into Hank's face. "You nearly did your own people in!"

Other men were shouting. Some were talking about hanging Hank. Perhaps, if he had not been such a loudmouthed bully and seeker of personal gain, his cowardice would have been pardoned; the situation had been terrifying enough to break a better man than Hank. But Hank could now expect little understanding from the other miners. They might indeed hang him.

Peterson stepped in and moved directly in front of Hank, who stared back at him with fearful eyes. "No, boys," Peterson said to the miners. "We haven't got a rope dirty enough to fit this coward's rotten neck."

There was muttering from the men. "We're giving you your life, Hank," Peterson said. "On one condition. That we never see hide nor hair of you again. Light out. And if we find you back in town, or anywhere near the mine, you'll be shot on sight."

Hank glanced wildly from Peterson to the angry men around him, wondering if this were some kind of trick. Let him go? But when he took a few hesitant steps away, and no one moved to stop him, he suddenly turned and ran out of the trench, followed by the jeers and catcalls of several of the men.

It was only when Hank had reached the top of the hill—relative safety—that some of his courage returned, in the form of his usual bluster. "You bastards ain't heard the last o' me yet!" he screamed, turning to face them, shaking his fist.

He had not considered what a fine target he made, standing in the open at the top of the hogback, outlined against the sky. It was not the miners who opened up on him, but several of the strikebreakers down by the train. Fortunately for Hank, the range was extreme and all the shots missed. But as bullets began to strike around him, he let out a yell, then turned and ran, disappearing out of sight over the crest of the hill.

Hank's speedy departure was so comical that the miners began to laugh. Good medicine, a way of breaking the terrible tension. The firing now stopped completely, with both sides, exhausted, eyeing one another warily.

"You think they're going to try again?" Peterson asked Gabe.

"Hard to say. I don't think they expected anywhere near this hard a fight. They've got a lot to think over."

Gabe was watching the train. He'd noticed activity around the two overturned stock cars. Suddenly, the one that was half up on the rails toppled over, falling clear of the tracks. They must have broken free whatever had been holding it in place.

And now there was considerable activity near the front cars, men moving along behind whatever cover they could find. "What's going on?" Gabe muttered.

"Hey! They're gettin' up steam!" a man yelled.

Sure enough, smoke was belching from the engine's smokestack; the engineer must have slipped back into the cab. The smoke increased. Steam billowed up around the engine, then suddenly the wheels began to turn. Backward.

"God!" a man bellowed. "They're pullin' out!"

Sure enough, the train was beginning to move backward, and men were pouring aboard the cars. A couple of the miners raised their rifles, ready for some parting shots, but others restrained them. "Let 'em go!"

The train picked up speed; in a few seconds it would be out of range.

"Do you think they're just trying to regroup?" Peterson asked Gabe.

Gabe shook his head. "I don't think so. I think they know they're beaten. At least for now."

Peterson looked glum. "Sounds like you think they'll be back."

Gabe shrugged. "Maybe, maybe not. Perhaps not this particular bunch. But somebody. The owners aren't going to give up after one fight. There'll be somebody coming for us, all right."

Peterson slowly nodded. "The army," he said softly. "The damned army."

"Yes. Probably."

CHAPTER EIGHTEEN

For several days after the defeat of the strikebreakers, the miners were exultant. All of them believed that in no time at all they'd be back working. Under much improved conditions.

But nothing happened. The mine owners back East refused to reply to the telegrams Peterson and his committee sent them. The owners were obviously just as determined to prevail as the miners.

There were rumors of the army being called in. The governor had sent representatives to town, demanding that the miners vacate the mine buildings and allow strikebreakers to enter. When the committee refused, the governor's men left angry.

The army. The thought struck fear in the minds of the men. A professional force brought against them. They would be fighting the republic. But still, the men continued to hang on.

Gabe had a different response to the prospect of meeting the army. He'd fought it many times before and was willing to do so again. He had old scores to settle, although he knew they could never be completely settled. How could he ever kill enough soldiers to make up for the loss of his wife and mother? For his friends who had been slaughtered?

But at least he could fight. The old cause had been lost when they'd moved the last of the tribes onto the reservations. He had a new cause now. Not as personal, but at least a cause.

Peterson, on the other hand, was horrified at the idea of fighting his country's army. "First," he explained to Gabe, "we can't win. Eventually we have to lose. Hell, you ought to know that more than anybody."

Gabe nodded. Over the past few days, he'd told Peterson a few things about his past. He had to admit that Peterson was right; in the end, you couldn't win. But for a while, you could fight like hell.

"In the second place," Peterson continued, "fighting the government puts us on the outside. Makes us look like criminals."

They were talking in the office of the former mine superintendent, who had lit out as soon as the fighting started. Peterson was pacing back and forth, while Gabe sprawled in an overstuffed chair. "Oh, I'll fight along with the rest, if it comes down to it," Peterson said. "We've gone too far to just give in tamely now. But if there were only some way to avoid that fight, some way to make the army hold back. . . ."

"Well," Gabe said, "I doubt you can shame it. You can't shame an organization that makes a practice of killing unarmed women and children. And as for scaring it, I suspect they're spoiling for a fight. There hasn't been much action for them lately."

"You're right," Peterson said, shaking his head ruefully. "We can't . . ."

He stopped pacing. "Hey, wait!" he said. "Maybe we can set it up so that if they fight, they lose. Even if they beat us."

Gabe looked inquiringly at Peterson, who was now grinning excitedly. "The mine," Peterson said softly. "This is all really about the mine, isn't it? About putting it back under the total control of those bloodsucking owners."

He turned to face Gabe. "What if there wasn't any mine? What if fighting would make the mine disappear? Then there wouldn't be much point in fighting, would there?"

"You thinking of performing a magic act?" Gabe asked. "Waving a handkerchief and making all those miles of tunnels disappear?"

"Maybe," Peterson said. "But not with a handkerchief."

He was smiling again. "Do you remember what it is that miners do so well?" he asked.

Gabe was still thinking when Peterson answered his own question. "We blast," he snapped. "We know how to blow things up."

Gabe had sworn to himself that he would never again go down into the mine. But now here he was, walking along one of the drifts with Peterson. Men were once again at work, drilling into the rock, setting charges. But these were not charges designed to break loose ore-bearing rock. These were charges designed to bring down the whole mine, cave it in on itself, close off the drifts forever. "Even if they take the mine back," Peterson explained, "they'll have a hell of a time getting it into working shape again. The way we're blasting, the whole place will be unstable. Sure, if they want to spend enough money, they might get it operating again someday. But they'll already have spent most of the potential profits, just to open a few drifts."

Gabe nodded, looking around at the men, watching the new energy with which they drilled into the rock. Even the big air drills, the widow-makers, were hammering away, filling the mine with their awful din.

It felt different, walking through the drifts as a free man. But it was still a mine, still dark and damp and incredibly hot. There were still millions of tons of rock sealing him off from the fresh air above. He hoped the army would want to fight, no matter what. It would be a good thing to shut down this miserable hole forever. No man should have to earn his living in such a place. Just for gold, the yellow metal that made the White Man crazy.

The day after the final charges were set, news came that the army was on the way, along with another group of strikebreakers, who were determined to use the army as a means of getting into the town. Then, the strikebreakers would take over the mine, and the miners would be thrown out, every one of them blacklisted. None of them would ever work in a mine again.

The strikebreakers arrived first. Once again their arrival was heralded by a distant plume of smoke, a train drawing near. Once again the miners rushed to their trenches overlooking the ruined railroad bridge. This time the train stopped well back, out of range of the trenches. Gabe was with Peterson in the top trench, watching as horses were unloaded from stock cars and men filed out of the cars. There were at least two hundred this time.

"I see Jennings," Gabe said to Peterson. He was watching the strikebreakers through binoculars. He panned a little further. "Damned if one of them doesn't look a hell of a lot like Hank."

"Here, let me see," Peterson said, reaching for the glasses. He steadied them on the edge of the trench. After a couple of minutes he said, "Yeah. Looks like him all right. Guess he sold us out. I'm not too surprised."

"He knows the trench layout," Gabe said. "By now, he'll have told everything he knows to Jennings. Otherwise, Jennings would have killed him straight off."

"Yeah. I wonder how much harm he can do us."

Gabe reached for his Sharps. "I can take care of it right now. The range is long, but if he keeps standing still . . ."

Peterson laid his hand on the Sharps's barrel. "No. They haven't started anything yet. There'll be time for Hank later."

Gabe sighed. Peterson had the damnedest habit of leaving his enemies alive. Someday one would kill him. But it was Peterson's show. At least, until Gabe was alone with Jennings. Then there would be some killing.

The strikebreakers seemed in no hurry to attack. They spent the next couple of hours unloading equipment from the train, an odd assortment of huge wheels, large metal sheets, and balks of heavy timber. It was only when they began assembling all this together that it became clear what they were doing. "They're making moving shields for themselves!" Peterson burst out. "Like in the Middle Ages."

Sure enough, the metal plates were being fastened to wheeled contraptions, which the strikebreakers would be able to push toward the trenches. Behind these shields, they would be safe from the miners' fire. "They'll be able to come right up to the bottom of the trenches," Peterson said worriedly. "And once they're in the trenches, we won't be able to use grenades against them without endangering our own men."

Gabe looked up at the sky. It would be dark in another hour. "I don't think they'll be done in time to attack today. Maybe some of our men can go out during the night and mine their approach."

Peterson brightened. "Yeah. Maybe."

The strikebreakers were still assembling their moving forts at nightfall. Both Gabe and Peterson agreed that a night attack was unlikely; the strikebreakers wouldn't be able to see the terrain well enough to keep from running their contraptions into holes.

As soon as it was dark enough, some of the miners left the trenches and crawled out onto open ground where they began setting dynamite charges into shallow holes. The men still in the trenches could hear faint sounds of digging. The strikebreakers were making so much noise banging away on their metal shields that they failed to hear anything at all.

"Well," Peterson said to Gabe. "It'll be tricky, setting off the charges at the right time. But maybe we'll at least slow them down a little."

Gabe slept in the trench, with both rifles close at hand. But dawn came without an attack. Most of the men, on both sides, had been sleeping. The sun was still behind the eastern hills when the strikebreakers began to assemble behind their contraptions. The attacking force spread out in a line about a hundred yards across. There were six of the moving forts, too few to completely cover all of the strikebreakers; some would probably hang back until the last minute. Watching through binoculars, Gabe could see Jennings walking up and down the line, checking each shield, probably telling the men what would happen to anybody who lost courage and ran. Gabe couldn't imagine Jennings thinking any other way.

Finally, just as the sun broke free of the mountains, sending its first bright rays down into the little valley full of men and metal, the strikebreakers began to move forward.

It did not go at all well. A wheel fell off one of the contraptions. The miners laughed as the strikebreakers struggled to get the wheel into place again. Another shield fell partly into a shallow depression. It took fifteen minutes to work it free. Obviously, Jennings meant for all six machines to come forward together, forming a solid front; each time one shield fell behind, the others waited.

They were just starting forward again, when Gabe, looking past Jennings and his men, saw a cloud of dust on the other side of a nearby hill. More strikebreakers? Then he heard a sound he'd hoped never to hear again, thin in the distance, but unmistakable. The sound of a bugle.

He nudged Peterson. "The army. They're coming."

Peterson turned pale. They might have been able to hold off the strikebreakers, at the cost of a lot of blood. But now, with the army reinforcing them . . .

They came around the hill and out onto the plain, a long line of horsemen, and behind them, the supply wagons. And with the wagons, four light field guns, bouncing and clattering along behind their limbers. Gabe pressed his lips together. He'd seen guns like that in action. Seen their shells blowing apart tipis, and those who lived inside the tipis. Seen the damage they could do. Even with the shelter of the trenches, casualties among the miners would be heavy.

The horse soldiers were moving at a canter now, outdistancing the wagons and guns, curving in a long arc. Gabe expected to see the soldiers and the strikebreakers coalesce into a group behind the shields, readying for a joint assault. He was surprised when the cavalry rode right out in front of the metal shields, putting themselves between the strikebreakers and the miners.

"What the hell's going on?" Peterson muttered. He and Gabe watched while one of the soldiers rode up to Jennings and dismounted. Gabe picked up the binoculars and studied the soldier. He was an officer. Stars glittered on his shoulders. Gabe turned to Peterson. "I'll be damned. They sent a general. I guess they figure this is pretty important."

Gabe and Peterson passed the glasses back and forth. Jennings and the general were talking. Shouting, probably, because Gabe could see Jennings waving his arms angrily. The general stood like a rock. Finally, he pointed toward his left. Gabe looked in that direction. He saw that the cannons had been unlimbered and were now pointed directly at the strikebreakers. Gabe put the glasses back on Jennings, saw him hesitate for a moment. Then Jennings threw down his hat in rage and stalked off.

"Well, I'll be," Peterson said softly. "He's callin' 'em off. Stopping 'em from attacking."

Gabe nodded. "I expect it'll be our turn next."

Sure enough, the general remounted, then rode straight toward the trenches. "Well, he's got guts," Peterson said. He rose up in the trench, calling down to his men, "Hold your fire! Let's hear what he has to say."

Peterson turned to Gabe. "Let's go." He started down the laterals. Gabe shrugged, then followed. They reached the bottom trench while the general was still picking his way over rough ground. Right over some of the dynamite charges. Peterson took the binoculars again and studied the general as he approached. "Son of a gun," he muttered. "It's General Evans. I met him once, back East. He's a decent man. Maybe we've got a chance after all."

The general stopped about forty yards from the trench, then dismounted. "I want to talk," he called loudly. "To whoever's in charge of this fool's comedy. If you've managed to agree on that much."

The general was not in a good mood. He'd had a hard, dusty ride, and he was not a young man. He tapped one foot impatiently against the ground as Peterson climbed up out of the trench. Gabe started to follow, but Peterson laid a hand on his arm. "No. One of us should stay behind. Just in case it's a trick."

Gabe nodded. He watched Peterson walk out into the open, Gabe slipped out of the trench and moved behind a low mound. He had the Sharps with him. If this *was* a trick, General Evans would never make it back to his lines alive.

Peterson stopped in front of the general. He said nothing. The general watched him for a moment, puzzled. Then he said, "Don't I know you? Some kind of lawyer feller?"

"I was a lawyer," Peterson replied. "Yes, we met once. Under more pleasant circumstances."

The general's face clouded. "What is all this, anyhow? Looks like you've got a regular war under way. You know we can't have that."

Peterson told him then about the mine, the terrible conditions, the owners' ruthlessness, the earlier attack by the strikebreakers. He talked him about the miners' determination to fight for what they felt was right and just.

When Peterson was finished, the general nodded his head. "Yes, yes, I can see your point. But you'd better see mine, too. We can't have private wars. That's why I've been sent here, to stop this damned fighting."

"You've been sent here, General," Peterson interrupted, "to put down the workingman. You know damned well that those Republican politicians who gave you your orders belong heart and soul to big business. They get bought at least once a day."

Evans suppressed a flash of anger. "I've always been sympathetic to the workingman," he finally said. "What the hell kind of stock do you think I came from? But as I just said, we can't have private wars. If there's going to be a war, I'll be part of it. So you make up your mind, mister. Pull out of those trenches now and throw down your arms, or we'll come in and dig you out. And you know we can do it."

Peterson nodded, his lips tight. "I'm sure you can, General. But, before the fighting starts, there's something I think you should know. Something that changes the entire situation for those money-grubbing assholes who got you ordered out here."

Peterson proceeded to tell him about the dynamite in the mine and how the mine would be destroyed if fighting started. Gabe, close enough to hear most of the words, saw surprise on the general's face. Then admiration. Finally, General Evans smiled. "You're a thinking man, Peterson. I like you. I'd hate to see you hang."

The general spent a moment scratching his chin. Finally, he spoke. "Okay, tell you what. One of the mine owners, name of Macaulay, the chairman of the board, is back a few miles, coming along in a train. If he wasn't here, I think I'd go ahead and attack, and to hell with both you miners and Macaulay's stinkin' mine. But with him so close, I'll let him make the decision . . . whether we blast you out of your holes or he settles with you."

With that, General Evens mounted his horse, pulled its head around, and rode away toward his own lines. Peterson remained in place for a few seconds . . . until he became aware of how exposed he was, standing in the open all alone.

He walked quickly back to the trench. Gabe was waiting. Peterson smiled tightly. "We got a chance, Gabe," he murmured. "If Macaulay has any brains at all. . . ."

CHAPTER NINETEEN

If Macaulay had any brains, they were immediately over-whelmed by his rage. He reached the area late in the afternoon. When General Evans told him about the ultimatum from the miners, he exploded. No bunch of ragged, Communist miners was going to tell him what to do with *his* property, *his* mine. He marched to a meeting with Peterson, the general alongside him. The three men met in approximately the same location where Peterson had earlier met with Evans. As before, Gabe hung back, his Sharps ready. He watched as Macaulay approached, a short, chubby man, overdressed for the region in a suit with a vest. Gabe's eyes flicked over the suit, then settled on Macaulay's face. A petulant face, with small features, a tight, pursed mouth, and greedy little eyes. Just about what he had expected.

There was no hesitation in Macaulay's manner. He marched right over to Peterson, looked up at the taller man, and barked, right off the bat, "I want you out of my mine, mister. Immediately!"

Gabe noticed that Peterson's expression remained impassive, determined. "Nice to have a chance to talk to you, Mr. Macaulay. We've sent a lot of messages your way, never got a direct reply."

"I don't talk to bandits," Macaulay snapped.

"We're not bandits, Macaulay," Peterson snapped back, dropping the "Mr." "We're the men who work your mine, make money for you. We let you know politely, a long time ago, about some problems we were having. Problems that would not have been that difficult to fix. Problems that affected our lives very deeply. Problems like how to remain alive in a mining situation that has no concern for the safety of the miners. Problems like a wage that will feed a man. . . ."

"Mister," Macaulay said, still not deigning to use Peterson's name, although he knew it well enough, "miners are a dime a dozen. If I listened to their constant whining, not an ounce of ore would be dug. If you and the bandits with you don't like the way I run my mine, you can pack up and leave. This is a free country."

"Yeah. With men like you owning all the work, we're free to starve. Uh-uh, Macaulay, we have to deal together, and we have to do it now. In a very real sense, it's our mine, too."

Macaulay's face reddened. He turned toward General Evans. "See!" he burst out. "What did I tell you? They're Communists. They're bringing that damned European Red talk right here into our country. That union shit. They—"

"We're not Communists, Macaulay," Peterson said coldly. "We're just men who want to be treated like men. Humans. We're gonna give you the same choice our people gave the British over a hundred years ago. Treat us like men, or you're gonna end up losing more than you can afford to lose."

General Evans was scuffing his feet, looking distracted. Macaulay looked like he was going to explode. "You think you've got me over a barrel, don't you?" he snarled. "Because you can blow up the mine. Well, let me tell you something, mister. Go ahead and blow it up. I'd rather lose it that way than get run over by a bunch of foreign-led traitors. So go ahead and blow it up. Then I'll see you dead, or in prison, Peterson."

There. In his rage, he'd finally used Peterson's name. Peterson smiled. Grimly. "Like our ancestors might have said, Macaulay, better dead fighting a bastard like you, than dying by inches in that hell you call a mine."

Macaulay had himself under better control now. "One last time, Peterson. Move away from the mine now. I'll even let you walk out of here alive. But you, and all the men who've sided with you, had better be out of here by morning. If not, then we attack. And if you blow the mine, you'll pay for it."

Now General Evans intervened. "I'll make any decisions about attacking, Macaulay. You move in those thugs of yours, I'll wipe 'em out."

He turned away from Macaulay to face Peterson. "And as for you miners, as far as the law is concerned, you're sitting on his property. I've been sent here to enforce the law. You've got until tomorrow morning to start pulling out. And if the mine blows, you'll be arrested, Peterson."

General Evans turned on his heel and walked away. Macaulay remained for a moment, glaring at Peterson. Then, realizing that he was all alone, within easy shot of the miners, he too turned and walked quickly after the general.

As Peterson walked back toward the trenches, anger, fear, and a little despair showed on his face. Gabe jumped down into the trench with him. "Damn," Peterson murmured. "I never figured the bastard would be so pigheaded. I really believe he'd rather lose the mine than give us a break."

"He keeps saying *his* mine," Gabe said. "I thought it had several owners."

"It does. But he's the chairman of the board. He owns most of the stock. His word is the final word."

They began walking up the laterals. "What are you going to do?" Gabe asked.

Peterson stopped and faced Gabe. "Me? I'm going to fight. And if the bastards attack us, I'm going to blow the mine. Even if I have to do it all by myself."

Peterson called a meeting of the most militant among the strikers. Gabe watched as Peterson told them everything that had happened, every word that had passed between himself and Macaulay. He let them know the stakes and the possible consequences, then asked them to go back to the men, most of whom could not leave the trenches, and ask them to vote on what they wanted to do.

An hour passed, during which Peterson paced back and forth as much as the narrow trench permitted. "I don't know if I have the right to ask them," Peterson murmured once to Gabe.

The men returned, gave him the miners' answer. Most would stay and fight. A few would be leaving. "We've gone too damned far to back out now," a burly driller told Peterson. "This is the first time in years that I've felt like a man."

So, as night fell, the men settled down to wait for the morning's showdown. Gabe and Peterson agreed that General Evans would do as he had said, use force if the men did not agree to at least lay down their arms. "But if we do," Peterson said, "Macaulay will have Jennings and his thugs all over us, sooner or later."

Gabe nodded absently. He had been watching the camp below. The soldiers had set up a neat bivouac flush against the wall of a low ridge. A hundred yards away, the strike-breakers had their own camp, a much more ragged affair, except for a big tent smack in the middle. Macaulay's tent. Gabe had watched while Jennings's men had set it up.

Macaulay. He was the key. Just as his stubbornness might destroy them all, a change of mind on his part could solve the entire problem. Gabe wondered what might cause Macaulay to change his mind. How could he be approached? How could he be influenced?

Gabe went over every bit of what had passed between Macaulay and Peterson. The more he thought, the more he became convinced that Macaulay had one particular weakness. And that weakness was precisely what others, Macaulay included, probably saw as Macaulay's greatest strength. Paradoxically, that weakness lay in his certainty, in his absolute

conviction that he was one-hundred-percent right, and in that
certainty, that nothing could actually threaten him. That he
stood so far above the fears and struggles of other men, that
nothing that touched them could touch him.

Well, Gabe reflected, maybe it was time for Mr. Chairman
of the Board Macaulay to discover just how human he was.
How vulnerable.

Gabe did not let Peterson know what he intended to do.
After it was dark, he left the trenches, walking back to where
the horses were being kept. His saddlebags were on the
ground, stacked with other gear. He opened his saddlebags
and took out a soft leather pouch. Carrying the pouch, he
did not head back to the trenches, but took a path that led
way around them to the right.

It took over half an hour to completely skirt the trenches,
but finally he moved down off the far right of the hogback
into a series of shallow gullies. A small spring, really just a
slow seeping of water, had formed in a low place. Making
certain that he was out of sight of everyone—the darkness
was fairly intense—he undressed, neatly stacking his clothing
on a flat rock. Then he opened the leather bag and took out
a breechclout, made of thin, supple leather, which he put
on. He reached into the bag again, took out some horn and
bone containers. They contained various pigments. What the
White Man often called war paint.

Mixing the pigments with the water, it took Gabe another
half hour to apply them both to his face and his body. The
body paint was for camouflage, to make him as invisible as
possible, to help him blend in with the night. The face paint
was another matter. Bold patterns, to inspire fear.

Finally, he was ready to move. He left the gully and
headed toward the enemy camp. The only weapon he took
with him was his knife, worn in a leather sheath tied around
his waist.

At first he was able to walk upright, but as he drew nearer
to his objective, he crouched lower, moving smoothly from
shadow to shadow. Finally, as he came within reach of the

faint glow of light emanating from the two camps, he dropped
down onto his belly and began to crawl.

His route took him close to the army camp. He could see
the soldiers. Some were still lounging in front of their little
two-man tents; others had their feet sticking out the ends,
already asleep. How tempting to slip into the camp and cut
a few throats, let the survivors find, in the morning, their
comrades lying dead next to them. For a moment hatred
almost overcame Gabe. He made a huge effort to control
himself. He was not here for revenge against the army. Few
of the men here tonight would even have been in the army
when his wife and mother were killed. But a few had been,
the older men. Perhaps some of the soldiers in this camp
had killed Indian women and children.

He crawled past the army camp. In a way, its neatness and
order made it less dangerous. Now he was approaching the
camp of the strikebreakers. Its very disorder meant increased
danger. Men roamed about aimlessly. Some were drinking.
It would be difficult to predict their movements, where they
might wander.

It took him an hour to crawl the last fifty yards. Once, a
man staggered out of a tent over to a clump of scraggly brush
where Gabe was lying, only half-hidden. The man, drunk,
vomited into the bushes, his vomit spattering onto the ground
only a foot from Gabe's right leg. If the man hadn't been
drunk, if he had been more alert, not so confident that the
army would protect him and his mates from the miners, he
might have noticed Gabe, might have seen the slight gleam
of light reflecting off his skin.

But the man finally turned and staggered back toward his
tent, groaning with sickness. Gabe, who had been lying
absolutely motionless, willing himself to be a bush, a rock,
a patch of grass, finally let out his breath.

He continued on until he was only a few feet from
Macaulay's tent. It was a big tent, brand-new, made of heavy
canvas. All around it the ground was open, with no cover at
all. Light from other tents gave a feeble illumination, enough

to make crawling across those last few feet impossible; he'd be seen. So Gabe, gauging the correct moment, when a burst of laughter from another tent drew general attention, simply stood up and walked around behind Macaulay's tent.

He crouched again, lay on his side, and looked under the flap of the tent. The interior was dimly lit. One candle guttered slowly on a tabletop. Papers were scattered all over the table. A hand came out of the gloom beyond the candlelight and picked up a paper. Then Macaulay's face appeared. He was sitting on the far side of the table, slowly going over the papers.

Gabe drew his knife and inserted the point into the canvas about a foot and a half above the ground. Slowly, very carefully, trying to work only when there was noise from the other tents, Gabe opened a slit in the tent's side. Then, just as slowly, he began to worm his way inside. The lighting helped; Macaulay had trouble seeing past the candle into the tent's far corners. Besides, he was intent on the papers.

The table was only a couple of feet wide. Slowly, Macaulay became aware of a subtle alteration of shadows on the far side of the table. At first he thought that it was the wavering flame of the candle. Then, to his amazement and horror, he realized that he was looking into a face, only a couple of feet away. A savage face, smeared with a pattern of lines and dots. Glaring at him from out of that face was a pair of almost colorless, absolutely cold eyes.

By the time Macaulay's stunned body was ready to react to this horrifying apparition, Gabe had moved to the other side of the table, spinning Macaulay around by one elbow, standing half behind him, with the blade of his knife lying cold along Macaulay's neck. "If you cry out," Gabe said softly, menacingly, "I'll cut your throat."

Macaulay made a gagging sound. He really did not know if he'd even be able to call out; his mouth and throat were suddenly very dry. The cold steel against his neck felt as if it were burning him. He turned his head slightly, found himself staring into those terrible eyes again and quickly looked away. "Who . . . who are you?" he finally managed to whisper.

"Death," the answer came, cold, without inflection.

"But . . . why?"

"If you're dead, then there won't be any point in the army attacking tomorrow. They'll want to get in touch with your . . . survivors. Ask what they want to do. Time will be gained. Perhaps some of the others won't be as . . . rabid as you."

"You're . . . from them? Peterson sent you?"

"No. I'm here on my own. Let's just say that I . . . sympathize with the miners."

Macaulay's mind was beginning to work a little more clearly. Craftiness began to do battle with his fear. "But if you kill me, it'll be blamed on them anyhow."

Gabe feigned hesitation. "Perhaps," he finally said. Then his voice grew harder again. "But you'll be dead. That's a good thing in itself."

"Why?" Macaulay cried.

"Because you think of men as dogs. No . . . worse than dogs. As machines, to be used up until they quit working. A man like you should not be permitted to live."

The certainty in Gabe's voice turned Macaulay's stomach into lead. He flicked his eyes to the side, caught another glimpse of that painted face, the terrible, remorseless eyes, so close to his own face. "Can't we talk about it?" he pleaded.

"About what? You've already made your decision. You're willing to lose the mine to gain your point. To crush good men."

The knife point moved a little higher, pricking under Macaulay's chin. "Maybe I was hasty!" Macaulay said quickly. "I was angry. People like Peterson . . ."

He felt the knife point change again, this time moving away. He moved his head gingerly. "Maybe this whole thing needs more time. I could agree to talk to Peterson. See if we . . ."

Gabe manufactured just the slightest suggestion of hesitation. Although, if this greedy pig did not do as he wanted him to do, he would certainly kill him. "You will not just talk," Gabe said abruptly. "You will tell the general, in the morning, that you agree to what the miners have asked for. You will deal with them in good faith. You will sign papers saying this. And then we will have peace again."

The knife rose higher, drew a drop of blood from just under Macaulay's jawline. "Do you understand?" Gabe snapped.

"Uh . . . yeah," Macaulay grunted, holding his chin high, away from the knife.

"You will do it?"

"Yes. Yes, I'll do whatever you say!"

The knife moved away from his throat. Macaulay raised a hand, massaged his neck, felt the slickness of his own blood on his fingertips. He started to turn, but Gabe abruptly spun him all the way around, so that their faces were only inches apart. Macaulay recoiled, trying to move away from those eyes, but Gabe held him fast. "You think you can promise anything now, then do the opposite once I'm gone. That is not true. Tonight, I came for you through a camp of alert soldiers. I passed through two hundred armed strikebreakers, guards, your men. It would be so much easier to find you in a city, to come into your home, into your bedroom, stand over your bed, wait for you to wake up . . . for the last time. Because, if you betray your own promise, then my promise will come to pass. My promise is this: I will find you, wherever you are, and cut your head off."

Macaulay's mind had already been racing, thinking how easy it would be to repudiate the promises this savage had extorted from him. But now, with those powerful hands once again at his throat, those eyes boring into his own, smelling the man's naked body, feeling the heat of him, listening to the absolute certainty in his voice, Macaulay nearly fouled his pants. Yes, this . . . creature *would* come for him. And nothing would be able to stop him. "I promise," he said weakly.

Gabe shoved him away. Macaulay spun and fell half over the table.

Macaulay fought to get his breathing under control, to keep from vomiting. "I'll pay you money," he blurted out. "Anything you ask. Just . . . stay away from me."

No answer. Filled with dread, Macaulay slowly turned around. There was no one there! The man had faded away as silently as he had come. Which Macaulay found the most frightening of all. So frightening that he was unable to call out, unable to raise the alarm, because if he did, he was certain that, like sorcery, he would once again be looking into those eyes. And this time there would be no mercy.

CHAPTER TWENTY

In the morning, everyone, the soldiers, the strikebreakers, even the miners, were awakened by the brisk notes of reveille. Slowly, the various players began to prepare for a day of decision; the miners rising, stiff and chilled, in their damp trenches; the soldiers performing their regular morning routines; the strikebreakers searching for a morning bottle to overcome the hangover from the night before.

Gabe and Peterson watched as the army broke camp, striking their tents, forming into ranks. "They're getting the cannons ready," Peterson said glumly. Sure enough, the gunners were swabbing out the bores and ramming home charges. Probably canister, which would be set to explode right above the trenches.

Horses were being saddled. Gabe figured that General Evans, keeping the miners pinned down by cannon fire, would sweep around their position, then attack from the rear, from the direction of the town.

Apparently Macaulay had said nothing to the general. He'd had an entire night to get over his fear. Too bad. Now a lot of men were going to die. Gabe would do his best to make certain that Macaulay was among them.

First, the parley. General Evans was already striding toward the area where he'd met with Peterson the day before, this time accompanied by several men, mostly soldiers. Gabe noticed that Macaulay was with the general.

Peterson stood up. "Well, let's go down and get the word," he said glumly.

This time Peterson took several of the miners with him, a show of unity among the men. He and his group left the trenches and walked out into the open. Gabe was with them, this time carrying his Winchester rather than the Sharps. They stopped and waited. The general and his entourage and Macaulay stopped a few yards away. The general got right to the point.

"Well, Peterson? You ready to give up this foolishness? Or are men going to have to die?"

"Men have *already* died, General," Peterson replied acerbically. His eyes tracked onto Macaulay, who was standing a few feet to the general's right. "It's up to you, Macaulay. Are you willing to at least listen to us?"

Macaulay hesitated. He was haggard; he had hardly slept. All night he had expected the savage to reappear next to his cot, knife in hand. In the morning he had started to go to the general, to tell him he had changed his mind, that he was going to give in to the miners. He even got as far as standing in front of Evans, but the words stuck in his throat. Negotiate with a bunch of anarchists? Betray the sanctity of property rights? Not possible. Not at all possible.

His resolve strengthened while he watched the army prepare for battle, saw Jennings readying his own sorry crew of cutthroats. Realizing that all this armed might was here to back him up reconfirmed his belief in the rightness of his point of view. The workingman was a dangerous animal that had to be kept in its place.

His resolve lasted right up to the point where the two sides met, especially when Peterson turned toward him, once again mouthing his outrageous demands. Macaulay's temper began to heat up. He was about to open his mouth, damn Peterson to hell . . .

Then he saw the man. Saw Gabe, standing a little behind Peterson, a rifle in his hands. The man last night had been nearly naked, his body and face covered with war paint. This man was fully clothed and his face was clean. But his eyes. They were the savage's eyes, cold, remorseless, boring straight into his own. Eyes so light that they barely seemed to have any color at all. Macaulay remembered those eyes only inches from his own. He remembered the promise of death they held. And now those same eyes were once again trapping his own. Macaulay stared at Gabe, tried to look away, but was not able to. And as Macaulay looked at Gabe, he realized, knew without a doubt, that nothing, not the army nor a hundred private guards, could keep this man from killing him if he went back on the promise he'd made the night before.

Macaulay became aware that someone was speaking to him. "Well?" the general was asking, rather curtly. "What about it, Macaulay? Aren't you at least going to answer the man?"

Macaulay gave a start, managed to tear his eyes away from Gabe's. "Huh? Ah, yes. An answer."

The usual words rose up in his throat. Words of condemnation. But he could not vocalize them. Instead, he heard himself saying, "General, realizing the gravity of the situation, I feel that some . . . negotiation is called for."

He realized they were all staring at him, the general rather blankly, Peterson with his mouth open. "I, uh, yes . . . negotiation," Macaulay continued. But then he remembered the savage's words, felt the cold steel against his throat again. An agenda had been specified. Macaulay glanced back toward Gabe, saw that he was still looking straight at him, his face impassive, but with death shining from those terrible eyes. "That is, I think we can accede to the majority of the men's demands, with some provisos, of course, such as the return of the mine, the removal of the dynamite."

Gabe smiled, a very slight smile, one that Macaulay didn't see, because he was now becoming locked into a dialogue with Peterson. It had worked, then. It had been a risk, but his gamble had paid off. He had not told Peterson what he'd done, had known that Peterson would not approve. How surprised Peterson looked. Better to be surprised than dead.

Gabe walked away. Let the lawyers haggle now, set terms, arrive at an agreement. As for himself, he'd be riding on soon. There was nothing more to hold him here.

He moved to the top of the revetments and looked down at the men grouped below. He watched as Jennings walked up to Macaulay and laid his hand on his shoulder to get his attention. Jennings's mouth was moving, probably asking what was going on.

Gabe picked up the binoculars and focused on Jennings and Macaulay. He saw the shocked look on Jennings's face when Macaulay started speaking to him. His shock turning to anger, Jennings argued with Macaulay until Macaulay dismissed him. Jennings, enraged, pulled off his hat and threw it onto the ground. The general scowled at him. Finally, Jennings stalked away, practical enough, however, to retrieve his hat.

Jennings. Still unfinished business. But Gabe would have to wait until this was all over. If he killed Jennings now, he might jeopardize everything Peterson had won. Maybe he would stay around just a little longer, see what developed.

Gabe left the trenches, retrieved his horse, and returned to his room in town. The town was practically empty. Gabe was looking out his window when the streets began to fill with the miners returning to their rooming houses, carrying their rifles as if they were now embarrassed by them. A little later the army rode down the main street, with the general, Macaulay, and Peterson at the head of the column. Macaulay looked up once and saw Gabe watching him from the window. The man visibly shrank in his saddle, jerked his eyes away, and hastily turned back toward Peterson.

Gabe watched Peterson and Macaulay go up the stairs to the superintendent's office. Two hours later, when Gabe finally left his room, hungry, the two men were just coming down the stairs. He watched as they shook hands. Gabe waited until Macaulay had left, then he walked up to Peterson. "Well, how'd it go?" he asked.

Peterson still seemed a bit shocked. "He agreed," Peterson said. "Agreed to practically everything that mattered. We've won, Gabe. And for the life of me, I don't know why. For a while I figured I must have misjudged Macaulay, but after a couple of hours with him, I'm even more convinced that he's a complete shit. However, for some reason, he seems determined to get along with us."

Gabe smiled. "Guess you can't fight success."

Peterson shook his head. "The funny thing is, I don't feel like I've won anything. I feel kind of . . . empty. I think what I'm trying to say, now that this is over, is that I have no interest in staying here. No interest in running a union. It was the doing that was important, not the having."

Gabe nodded. "An important thing for a man to realize."

"Yeah." Peterson said absently. "You know, I think I want to work as a lawyer again. Do this same kind of thing, but within the law. I've been hearing a lot about California lately, about Los Angeles, how the Mexican people there are being treated badly, cheated out of their land because they don't know the law. Maybe I could go there, do something for them, stick up for their rights."

Gabe smiled. Peterson was going to end up a politician after all. "Well," Gabe said, "I'm going to stick up for my stomach. I'm going over to the restaurant and get something to eat. Want to come along?"

But Peterson, still lost in thought, said that he wanted to go talk to some of the men, so Gabe went to the restaurant alone. There were not many men inside; most had returned to their rooms to get some sleep. If the negotiations went well, they'd be back in the mine soon. Working conditions might improve, but they would never improve enough to make a mine anything other than a mine.

Gabe was about halfway through a huge slab of steak when something outside caught his eye. A bearded miner passing by. Then it registered who that miner was. Hank! Walking purposely along the boardwalk, head down, his face a mask of hatred.

Gabe started to get to his feet, but just then the door crashed open and a figure appeared in the doorway. It was Jennings. Armed, as usual. And looking straight at Gabe. "Conrad!" he snarled. "I don't know how the hell you did it, but I got a gut feeling you engineered this whole goddamned sellout. You been bucking me from the start, but mister, it's time to pay up."

The few customers were scrambling to get out of the way. Gabe slowly sat back down, keeping both hands on the table. Jennings was to his right; Gabe would have to turn to face him, and he suspected that while he turned, Jennings would draw and fire. He was standing with his knees slightly bent, right hand near the butt of his pistol, ready to move, hair-trigger ready. His expression was cold, murderous.

"Well . . ." Gabe started to say, his voice hesitant.

"Shut your stinkin' yap!" Jennings snarled. "Go for your gun or . . ."

Jennings had fallen for it, given Gabe just that instant of inattention he had been looking for. Jennings had been working his mouth when he should have been concentrating.

Gabe had both hands on the table, his right hand brushing the edge of his plate. In one smooth move he sailed the plate straight at Jennings's face. Jennings instinctively ducked, clawing for his pistol, but he was off balance now, and Gabe had already reached across his body with his left hand. He rose into a crouch, with the muzzle of his pistol tracking toward Jennings.

The hammer was still uncocked, but his right hand was settling onto the butt, clamped over his left, his right thumb slipping the hammer back. He fired three fast shots, fanning the hammer with his thumb while holding the trigger back. Firing two-handed, he was able to hold down the recoil, keeping the bucking gun aimed straight at Jennings's chest.

Jennings got off one shot, but he was already staggering back under the impact of Gabe's bullets, clutching at the door frame with his left hand while the gun roared in his right, sending a bullet into the floor.

All three of Gabe's bullets struck in an area no more than six inches wide right in the middle of Jennings's chest. Jennings flew out the door, falling down the steps that led up to the restaurant, landing on his back on the gritty board-walk.

Gabe walked out of the restaurant and down the steps. Jennings was still alive, but barely. His pistol was in his hand. Gabe stepped on Jennings's wrist, pinning the pistol. Jennings looked up at him, tried to say something, but could not form the words.

It was hard to say when he died; his eyes continued to stare up at the sky even after he'd stopped breathing.

Suddenly, Gabe heard gunfire from further down the street. He remembered Hank. Jennings and Hank must have come into town together. For vengeance. And while Jennings had come for Gabe, Hank would be after Peterson.

Gabe broke into a run. More shots came from the superintendent's office. At least half a dozen shots.

Gabe was still forty yards away when Hank came staggering out of the office doorway, at the head of a steep flight of stairs. He had a gun in his hand, but from the way he was moving, he had been badly hit. Had he killed Peterson then?

No. Peterson now appeared in the doorway, holding a bloody shoulder. "Hank, you son of a bitch!" he shouted. Hank turned, tried to bring his gun up, but Peterson, steadying his hand on the banister, put two bullets straight into Hank.

Hank rolled all the way down the stairs, ending up in a heap on the boardwalk. Peterson followed him down. Hank was still alive. He tried to raise his gun. Peterson, standing over him, aimed carefully, then blew away half of Hank's head.

Peterson was leaning against the banister when Gabe walked up to him. The only wound Gabe could see was a scratch on his shoulder. Peterson looked up, his eyes still a little crazy.

"Well," Gabe said. "I see you finally figured it out."

"Huh?" Peterson muttered, his eyes steadying.

Gabe smiled. "Never leave an enemy alive."

A special offer for people who enjoy reading the best Westerns published today.

WESTERNS!

NO OBLIGATION

Mail the coupon below

To start your subscription and receive 2 FREE WESTERNS, fill out the coupon below and mail it today. We'll send your first shipment which includes 2 FREE BOOKS as soon as we receive it.

- -

Mail To: **True Value Home Subscription Services, Inc. P.O. Box 5235**
120 Brighton Road, Clifton, New Jersey 07015-5235

YES! I want to start reviewing the very best Westerns being published today. Send me my first shipment of 6 Westerns for me to preview FREE for 10 days. If I decide to keep them, I'll pay for just 4 of the books at the low subscriber price of $2.75 each; a total $11.00 (a $21.00 value). Then each month I'll receive the 6 newest and best Westerns to preview Free for 10 days. If I'm not satisfied I may return them within 10 days and owe nothing. Otherwise I'll be billed at the special low subscriber rate of $2.75 each; a total of $16.50 (at least a $21.00 value) and save $4.50 off the publishers price. There are never any shipping, handling or other hidden charges. I understand I am under no obligation to purchase any number of books and I can cancel my subscription at any time, no questions asked. In any case the 2 FREE books are mine to keep.

Name

Street Address   Apt. No.

City   State   Zip Code

Telephone

Signature
(if under 18 parent or guardian must sign)

Terms and prices subject to change. Orders subject
to acceptance by True Value Home Subscription
Services, Inc.

954-4